Praise for *Oslo, Maine*

"A Moosetagonist, a musician reluctantly teaching, neighbors with guns, neighbors with drug problems, neighbors whose kid owns a beautiful mind, a wealthy patron, a literal-minded simple scion, a lover, another, a husband, a violin: the other Maine. Marcia Butler has pulled all these elements and much more together into one sweeping tale of love and redemption, a lot of laughs along the way, and sorrow, too, flights of transcendence, an aria sung by a moose who knows more than the rest of us what it is to be alive. *Oslo, Maine* is richly satisfying, a book for a quiet afternoon, a cup of tea, music in the background. Don't mind that big soft nose at the window: the moose has come for you."

— Bill Roorbach, author of *The Girl of the Lake, The Remedy for Love,* and *Life Among Giants*

"How do we cope with the unimaginable? Maybe, says Marcia Butler, in her brilliant new novel, we do it with the unimaginable. When 12-year-old Pierre Roy loses his memory in an accident, three Maine families, a crosscut of cultures and classes, are at loose ends as to what to do. Instead, it's up to one boy and the incredible sound from one violin, to change and challenge everything everyone thought they knew. Gorgeously written and hauntingly told, Butler's novel, about love, forgiveness, and yes, coming to terms with our failures, is as breathtaking as Maine itself."

— Caroline Leavitt, *New York Times* bestselling author of *Pictures of You* and *Cruel Beautiful World*

D0030451

"*Oslo, Maine* is an enchantment; I read it in two sittings, utterly absorbed, spellbound by this world where everyone—even a mother moose—has secrets and hidden yearnings (and unexpected capacities), and where even damage can prove to be a redemptive gift. Marcia Butler is a master dramatist, a sorceress, and extraordinary novelist; this book will break your heart and heal it."

— E. J. Levy, author of *Love, in Theory* and forthcoming, *The Cape Doctor*

"Wildly plotted, astutely observed, and brimming with wit, *Oslo, Maine* briskly unfurls its central mystery, portraying a motley brand of Mainers with precision, and causing unsuspecting readers to become deeply invested in the plight of a moose and her calf. Marcia Butler explores the blunt, hard follies of human nature with verve and humor in this innovative and charming novel."

— Adrienne Brodeur, author of the national bestselling memoir *Wild Game*

"In her impressive new novel *Oslo, Maine*, Marcia Butler offers readers a seductive, imaginative, and utterly unique story; an astute and compassionate foray into the intersecting lives of characters who are both ordinary and exceptional, saintly and deeply flawed. I raced through this novel in one breathless sitting. Highly recommended!"

— Karen Dionne, #1 internationally bestselling author of *The Wicked Sister*

Praise for *Pickle's Progress*

"The four main characters in *Pickle's Progress* seem more alive than most of the people we know in real life because their fears and desires are so nakedly exposed. That's because their creator, Marcia Butler, possesses truly scary X-ray vision and intelligence to match."

— Richard Russo

"With detached wit and restrained horror at her characters' behavior, Butler explores the volatile nature of identity in this provocative novel."

— *Booklist*

"In this study of how childhood experiences shape perception, and how deception keeps people caged, Butler shows that nothing need be set in stone."

— *Kirkus Reviews*

"Marcia Butler is a gifted storyteller with a uniquely dry sense of humor."

— NPR

"Invigorating, sly and mordantly funny, *Pickle's Progress* offers a comic look at the foibles of human nature and all the ways love can seduce, betray and, ultimately, sustain us."

— Jillian Medoff, bestselling author of *This Could Hurt*

"A wild ride. A suicide, an Upper West Side brownstone, and twin brothers come together in this surprising and trenchant debut novel from memoirist Marcia Butler."

— *Vulture*

OSLO, MAINE

A NOVEL

MARCIA BUTLER

central
avenue
publishing

2021

Published by Central Avenue Publishing, an imprint of Central Avenue Marketing Ltd.
www.centralavenuepublishing.com

Published in Canada
Printed in United States of America

1. FICTION/Literary   2. FICTION/Small Town & Rural

OSLO, MAINE

Trade Paperback: 978-1-77168-231-2
Epub: 978-1-77168-232-9
Mobi: 978-1-77168-233-6

For Céleste-Marie Roy
Dearest friend
Then, now and always

OSLO, MAINE

PROLOGUE

ONE WEEK AFTER ARRIVING IN OSLO environs and before giving birth to her calf, the moose approached the Hump for the first time. The land mass was a longitudinal ridge that separated Oslo on the eastern slope from the Demarchelier Paper Mill, nestled in a valley to the west. Cresting at an altitude just shy of one thousand feet, the Hump conveniently prevented the mill's toxic runoff from invading Oslo water supply and the surrounding lakes. And except for an occasional rogue eastern downdraft, prevailing westerly air patterns held its pernicious smell at bay. With these conditions in place, Oslo, Maine remained a pleasant enough place to live and the March, as the paper mill was commonly known, had provided healthy blood flow to the town's economic heart for generations.

It was late April, and the sun had begun its descent behind the White Mountains to the southwest in New Hampshire. Though the moose had poor eyesight, especially with regard to distance, she noticed a patch of birch trees high on a barren ridge, whose virgin leaves shimmered against the waning light. She'd been foraging all day and the climb would take considerable energy, but the moose was still hungry, the calf inside her active. She summited the Hump and fed efficiently by stripping several trees of spring buds.

Now full dusk, the temperature dropped quickly, causing the moose's skin to ripple from the chill. She navigated down the western slope, stepping around stubby brush and through residual patches of winter snow until she reached the bottom. This side of the Hump appeared mostly devoid of edible plants and trees, though a nearby patch of fronds presented as a suitable bed. Just as she prepared to collapse her legs and lie for the night, she heard a familiar trickle. She approached the sound, which proved to be a stream, and placed one hoof in the water to test the depth. Satisfied that the stream was shallow, she extended her neck down to drink. The water gave off an acrid stench, and she quickly recoiled with aversion. This sudden reaction set in motion a chain of events.

Something brushed her head—a tickle at her ears. She heard a series of snaps and simultaneously, something that resembled a snake dropped over her head, encircling her neck. Startled, she backed away but was unable to move more than a foot. Walking forward into the putrid water also proved impossible. Spreading her four legs at slight angles in order to stabilize the weight of herself and her calf, she began to thrash her head back and forth, up and down. The snake-thing tightened all the more.

The moose, possessing exceptional hearing, rotated her ears in an attempt to locate other animals. But the area exuded a malevolent quiet—dangerous, because she'd never encountered this particular predator throughout her twenty years in the natural world. And her strange captor seemed to operate with a native intelligence. It had managed to scoot up her long neck, past the dewlap, and was now tight at the cusp of her throat. She worked her tongue from side to side, attempting to swallow, but could only bark a cough brought on by the sustained constriction. Very soon, saliva frothed at her lips and stiff hairs rose up on her shoulders and spine. The moose had entered a full panic.

Over the course of the next hour, the moose made many attempts to free herself. She alternately strained mightily and then eased up when exhausted. Sustained moans, meant to attract other moose as far away as two miles, went unheeded. Finally, she gave herself over to capture. And once she ceased struggling altogether, the snake-thing slackened its tension at her neck, almost as a reward for relinquishing all efforts to escape. There, standing at the lip of the stream, the moose and her unborn calf managed an uneasy sleep.

Dawn broke. No other animals approached the stream as would be normal in the early hours, the water source surely known to be non-potable. If birds nested nearby, they remained silent. Indeed, as the sun rose in a cloudless sky, a barren land spread out before the moose. Bushes and trees appeared dwarfed, like in the dead of winter, rather than flourishing with buds as would be expected in spring. Any snow that remained was covered with black silt encrusted across the surface. The moose, now fully awake to this strange landscape, felt a fresh urge to free herself. She recycled pointless movements and made weak calls to other animals. Her calf kicked at intervals, but before long went unnaturally still.

Soon, thirst became her most pressing need. Though the stream was foul, the moose made one more massive attempt to get water down her throat. She pulled against the snake-thing and managed to poke her snout a few inches into the water. Not only did her throat close up again, but overnight her tongue had swollen to almost twice its normal size, which rendered her incapable of swallowing. So whatever water did manage to seep into her mouth went nowhere. This was a bewildering confluence of restrictions she'd never known before. And as if to punish her further, the moose urgently, now more than ever, wanted to collapse to the ground. Yet each time she sank, the choking around her neck thwarted that need.

In early afternoon, just as the moose had managed to relax into another dozing state, a noise from behind startled her. She was unable to turn her head, but recognized the sound as one she'd encountered near the paths on which humans traveled. The grinding noise grew in volume and stopped directly behind. The sound of four slams and approaching footsteps shook her.

"It's a moose cow. A beauty."

"Seems like she's been here for what—maybe a day? Look at her scat."

Humans were not the moose's natural predator. Though worthy of caution, especially when she had a calf in tow, in most cases their presence wouldn't feel particularly menacing. Only packs of wolves had success killing her kind. But now, being trapped, the moose had no choice but to tolerate their touch. Hands slid down her legs then back up to her withers. Fingers traced the deep scarring across her flank, a vestige of surviving a decade-old battle with wolves. She felt pressure around the dewlap at her neck. The humans probed and squeezed everything. When they rubbed the fur at the moose's belly in circular motions, her calf responded with a weak kick.

"Wow, she's pregnant. Claude's gonna flip over this."

"Yeah, a bonus for sure. Let's get her hooked up and walk her to the March."

"Nice and easy, boys. Claude won't want her stressed. Keep that meat tender."

Up until that point the moose had not seen the humans; she'd only heard their soft calls and felt their touch. Now, for a brief moment, one set of hands flickered in front of her eyes and just as quickly, everything went dark. A softness shrouded her head, and her sight could not adjust as it would at night. Before her was an impenetrable black. Nature did not know this hue.

The men drove around to the front of the moose and tethered her to ropes connected to winches at the back of the truck. Slowly but insistently, they pulled her about a half mile toward a loading dock no longer in use. This section of the March, permanently closed due to downsizing, sat at the westernmost side and was not visible from the Hump or any approaching road. The surrounding asphalt, which in previous years had been a parking area, was overrun with unruly grass and saplings that barely flourished now only as weeds. They parked a few hundred yards from the building, then sat in the truck for several minutes to watch the moose gradually settle down. Once she seemed acclimated, they got out of the truck, leaving the doors open so as not to startle her. Now they'd begin the most challenging aspect of the capture—to work calmly and swiftly, yet with precision.

The men unspooled four ropes from the truck. With one end clipped to a large metal ring attached to the noose at the moose's withers, they wrapped the opposite ends around their waists. Then, positioning themselves at four corners around the moose, they stretched the ropes taut so as to equalize the torque differential. With the larger captures, the goal was to distribute the weight and drag the animal up the loading ramp and into the building in one motion. Since Claude had begun the trapping business about a year back, they'd developed this specific method through trial and error. Now with everything secured, the men began that final pull.

The moose noticed a change in the air. The humans, while moving around her, discharged their musky scent, which she'd often encountered when roaming near their structures. But the sounds, chinking and snapping, were completely foreign to the moose. As she tried to sort out what she was hearing, her body was pulled, oddly, from many directions at once. And because she was still blinded, the moose had no choice but to allow the conflicting pressures to propel her forward as grunts from the humans peppered the air.

Suddenly she was up a slight incline, and a chilled stagnation swathed her body. It was as if the air had collapsed onto her head or had vanished altogether. Just as quickly, a great shattering noise from behind caused an uncomfortable pressure in her ears. She felt a flutter at her head and the soft darkness lifted. As her eyesight adjusted, she glanced toward a light source above and was surprised by multiple stars very close to her body, organized in a regular pattern she'd never seen in the sky. The moose looked down and found herself standing on impossibly hard earth, without the natural give of soil. It was then that the moose began to notice not so much what was present, but what was lacking: a distant sky above, grass, trees, hills. No horizon at all. But as disorienting as all this was, what shook her most was what she smelled: urine, defecate, and other gore, all of which seemed to embed deep into her nostrils. She snorted to try and release the foulness but could not expunge the odor. Here, she knew, animals had been in trouble. They had not escaped. This place held death.

"What should we do with her?"

"Wait for Claude, for sure. But it looks like she's real close to birthing."

"He'd want them both healthy. Let's give her water."

"Good idea. That'll sustain them pretty well for another day until the slaughter."

She felt a human pat the fur by her calf. The snake-thing went slack, and though her movement was somehow still restricted she was now able to move her head up and down. As the moose gingerly tested this marginal freedom, a human came into view and placed something on the ground at her front legs. She leaned down and poked her nose into the liquid. It was fresh and cold and greatly needed; the moose began to drink. As soon as she finished, more water appeared, again and again. Soon she felt quenched and her calf, too, began to move in response to the hydration.

The humans left, their sounds and smells disappearing to somewhere she could not imagine. After a time, the moose became accustomed to the chill of the room, the hard ground, and the air, thick and moist. She began to look around. Snake-things lay by the walls, limp, perhaps even dead. Those walls, all dark red and brown, were smattered with blood and offal speckling the surfaces. The many round stars in the false sky felt even more ominous with their unnaturally close proximity and strong glow. Never before had she known such a lack of natural things. And soon, the moose was aware of another presence surrounding her—ghosts of dead animals, their eyes pooling with wet and their mouths open yet making no sound.

SOME TIME LATER, the moose woke from a doze to a different light, warm and familiar, spreading against her from behind. Wind blew, a welcome diffusion of the deathly smells. A small human ran all around, circling her, darting here and there. She saw red fur on its head as it jumped up and down in front of her. It made repeated high-pitched squeals.

"No, Luc! No! *Luc*!"

"Oh, Mother of Jesus. Pierre! Get away from her!"

"She's trapped!"

"I said get away from that thing, Pierre. It's dangerous."

"Please, Luc. I know we can save her!"

The small human left the moose's view. Then she felt it take hold of her tail with a modest grip and push against her backside. The moose instinctively released her scat. The small human shrieked again, now louder and sustained, and clamped on to her tail with greater strength. A large human with black fur appeared at her side and roughly yanked on the long snake-things which had kept her from moving. Then she felt intense pressure into her flank as the large human with black fur attempted to turn her around. Simultaneously, the small human took hold of one of her back legs. Suddenly the idea of potential escape made the moose go wild. She raised both hind legs, and with the small human still attached, bucked with massive force. A dense thud. Then silence.

With nothing to constrict her for the first time in many hours, the moose took in this terrible place. In a corner, the small human with red fur was folded into a lump. The large human hovered above the small one as it quivered and began to moan. But the moose spent no more than a few seconds on these visions. Because ahead of her was the color of freedom: the blue of a natural sky.

She took off at a speed rarely needed and flew across the asphalt, her hoofs trampling weeds that barely thrived. Her calf remained still, as if to allow the moose to expend all her energy on their escape, and in no time she reached the area of initial capture. She brought her pace to a walk and saw all the dangers from the night before: the water she could not drink and the well-disguised contraption that threw the snake-thing over her head, which now looked to have colluded as dual enemies. She stood at a safe distance, saw all her mistakes, and absorbed this new knowledge. When she came upon the fronds she almost slept on—and would have done so had she not been thirsty—the western side of the Hump rose in front of her. In her still-weakened state, the moose considered the difficult climb and the easier descent that would bring her to a secluded place where, in just a few days, she would birth her calf.

Now, a new sound intruded—first from far away, then increasing in volume. A loud, staggered wail. She saw a large metal container with flashing colored stars speeding, speeding, speeding, heading toward the place of death where she'd injured the small human with red fur. Without hesitation, the moose scrambled up the Hump, crested the barren ridge, and descended toward a town in central Maine the humans called Oslo.

THE WORDS

CLAUDE ROY RETRACED HIS STEPS, LOPING back down a few dozen yards on the dirt path to discover his son on his hands and knees. A steady rain the night before had caused mush. That, and late-May snow melt, left much of the soil generally sloppy, which then made for unsure footing for the skinny twelve-year-old. Claude slid to a halt and toed Pierre's forehead. The boy offered his face—a galaxy of freckles strewn across his cheeks, a mop of bright-red hair currently in need of a barber—and gave up a guileless smile that not a soul in Oslo could resist.

This was the third such disruption Pierre had caused since they'd begun this Saturday-morning hike. As that specific number—three—crossed his mind, Claude realized with halfhearted shame that he'd been keeping count. It would've been simple enough if they'd navigated the trail side by side, so he might help Pierre recover when he lost his footing, or simply hold the boy's hand, for God's sake. Actually, an unhurried stroll would have made even more sense, because Claude was six foot four and Pierre hadn't yet reached five feet, the physics of stride inequity clearly at play. But Claude, an impatient man by nature, couldn't seem to toggle himself to Pierre's gait. He'd set and maintained a good lead the minute they breached the woods. This then dangled the obvious question: why hike together at all? Claude had to admit his pace bordered on sadistic.

Pierre scrambled to his feet, swatting moist dirt off his pants as best he could. His Keystone 22 rifle had been tossed to the side of the path and lay precariously close to a puddle. Increasing the potential for even more damage, a persistent breeze had blown leaves and debris across the weapon. Bile shot up Claude's throat. Before they'd left the house, he'd warned Pierre to make certain that dirt, water, or any crap whatsoever didn't muck up the mechanism. Protecting a firearm at all costs was a hunter's mantra, he'd added at the end of his lecture. But Claude managed to swallow his irritation and made an about-face, leaving Pierre to wipe down the rifle on his own. In less than a minute the boy caught up and, walking behind him, curled his fingers around Claude's belt. Claude felt Pierre's knuckles rub against his lower back. The contact was welcome and seemed to erase the last five minutes.

"A squirrel!" Pierre screamed his fondness for pointing out the mundane.

"*Rapture*," Claude whispered, loud enough to elicit a giggle from Pierre, whom he knew also appreciated hyperbole.

As if having negotiated a tentative truce, they trudged further into the woods, aiming for a familiar rock on which they'd sit and take their lunch. The quiet between them gave Claude time to mull over the specific disappointments he felt with regard to his son.

Weak. It came too easily, not tempered by any mitigation through deliberation, and the truth of it made Claude wince. This, he knew, was a term no father should bandy about in his head, not to mention roll over his tongue, and surely not about his preadolescent child. But he worried for Pierre, because never in his life had Claude seen a man emerge with his masculinity intact when operating from an intrinsic state of weakness. Bluster, even faked arrogance, provided no effective mask. If all this was true, Claude surmised, his boy just might be doomed.

The previous evening, during an ongoing fracas he and his wife had waged virtually every night since Pierre's accident at the March a month prior, Claude tripped hard on that word. *Weak.* Celine went feral, like a filly being broken with a harsh rein. Her mouth formed a rictus so ugly it scared Claude, and he couldn't imagine what was headed his way—howling for sure, maybe even violence. Celine had exhibited mercurial moods of late, which Claude knew was due to the stress of Pierre's injury. But to his surprise, and then relief, she'd backed off abruptly. Tucking a tear-stained pillow under her head, she explained to Claude as if *he* were the child, that "weak" was not a kind, or even accurate, characterization of *her* son. Claude, of course, noted the possessive pronoun used to emphasize her belief that he was incapable of understanding *their* child. As an alternative, she lobbed "sensitive" from across the room. But Claude didn't like that word, either. In fact, it was much worse. It chafed at him as feminine, which was murky territory he was loath to go anywhere near, particularly with regard to his only progeny. Because what would that then mean about Claude himself, the lamb not being so far from the goat, or some such adage? So, they continued to fling synonyms at each other and finally, long past midnight, managed to compromise on "quirky," which was a compliment, to Celine's mind, and nebulous enough for Claude to acquiesce to, at least at that late hour. With that wrinkle pressed out Celine was snoring within minutes, leaving Claude, slumped in a chair by the window, to watch the sun rise.

After about a quarter mile Claude felt Pierre's hand slip from his belt, but the boy kept up this time, panting with the effort. This pleased Claude, though listening to him slap his bare arms nonstop because of mosquitos annoyed him with equal measure. He'd advised Pierre to wear a long-sleeved shirt for just this reason, but to no avail. Pierre had listened to the weather report the night before and with predicted warming temperatures, he'd insisted on wearing a T-shirt under his orange hunting vest. Claude kept an "I told you so" admonishment to himself, and Pierre suddenly sped ahead, rounded a corner, and was soon out of sight.

Now Claude basked in what he imagined only the thick woods of Maine could give him. Not so much the cliché of being alone with nature. Rather, the idea that if he ended up alone, he might be okay with that. And somehow, the protection of a thick canopy of birch trees dappling sun across his face gave Claude the camouflage needed to muse about what he assumed all men of middle age must consider from time to time. A secret and frightening contingency plan: that single life would be easier than toughing out the complexities of those he professed to love most in the world. Which then led him to recall, again, how seriously difficult and headstrong Celine had behaved the night before. Not to mention all the words she'd thrown at him in the privacy of their bedroom. Weak. Sensitive. Special. Emotional. Perceptive. Soft. Delicate? *No.* All unacceptable. Then, the fatal personality modifier: *quirky.* She'd been able to jam that one down his throat due, in part, to his exhaustion from having just worked a double shift at the March. Also, the fact that Celine understood all too well that Claude was never at his best at three a.m. But now, feeling more clearheaded from the pot of coffee he'd mainlined before he and Pierre had set off, Claude wasn't so sure about that word. In fact, the more he thought about it, *quirky* actually irked him quite a lot. Because Pierre's most disturbing quirk to date ate Claude alive.

Books. They'd abducted his son with stealth and breathtaking speed from the day he'd started kindergarten. Claude and Celine hadn't come from families of readers by any measure, so this was not some quaint tradition handed down through generation or gene pool. And despite Catholic backgrounds, Celine, and Claude to a greater degree, didn't believe in a higher power. So the mighty hand of God was not at work here. But as Pierre's passion for reading grew to what Claude deemed unnatural, he couldn't help but entertain the notion that this might be the work of some devil who'd invaded his son. For all of Oslo, Pierre was an entertaining sideshow. For Claude, an embarrassment.

The boy was cued up at the library till the end of days, or so repeated the head librarian whenever she'd bump into Claude at the hardware store, a frequent haunt for them both. He noticed she'd bought a lot of PVC piping and suspected she was trying to plumb her own house, which of course was illegal. At the point when he couldn't tolerate one more soliloquy on Pierre's to-be-read list (projected to the highest shelf, stocked with, poetically, drain cleaner), he'd rerouted the conversation to toilets and building codes. That shut her down nicely. In the end, the librarian's shoddy plumbing would remain their little secret, and Pierre's book fetish, mercifully, became a closed subject. But that was a mere private squabble at the hardware store, and easily buried. What Claude couldn't control was Pierre's habit of devouring his books publicly, sometimes while walking. On any given day the boy could be observed walking up and down the aisles at Shaw's supermarket—from dry goods to frozen foods to the dairy aisle—with his nose between the pages. He never looked up. Not once. His ability to sidestep cereal, fish sticks, lampposts, vehicles, people, *whatever*, unnerved Claude no end. Pure delight for Celine.

Claude double-timed and caught up with Pierre. After dropping their gear on a dry patch of ground, they sat on the family rock, nicely warmed by a noon sun. The Spam, tomato, and mayo sandwiches Celine had prepared the night before were consumed in a matter of minutes. Claude took a swig of coffee from a thermos and felt the fresh rush of caffeine. As he lay back on the rock and closed his eyes, he heard a few birds pecking about nearby. The steady breeze cut into the sun's heat. And it all felt fine for the moment. Because by surrendering to the daily work of critters and the way of nature, Claude also managed to curb taking additional mental inventory of Pierre, which had saturated his thoughts since the day had begun. With this mental reprieve he felt his chest ease, as if he'd been holding his breath since dawn.

Claude opened his eyes and saw that Pierre had also stretched out, close enough to smell his sweet-and-sour sweat. From this vantage point, he could see the pug nose Pierre had inherited from Celine, and his own father's slightly pigeon-toed feet. Claude wondered what *he* had given Pierre and then realized he wished, more than anything, that his son would eventually grow an impressive physique, just like his. Claude was tall and lean, sporting at least a four-pack—a formidable sight from any distance. Once in a while Celine told him his face was nicely proportioned, which he assumed was a compliment. And his brown-black hair hadn't gone grey in the least. The side part in Pierre's hair was near, and Claude reached over to brush away some dandruff from his peach scalp. He meant it as a benign gesture, but Pierre shoved Claude's hand away and quickly ejected from the rock to busy himself with gathering up the trash, of which there was very little. Purell appeared and Pierre squirted it liberally on his palms, rubbing longer than was needed. His son was stalling.

"Get out the bullets, just like we went over at home," Claude instructed, still staring at the sky from his reclined position.

"Right. But I forgot my earplugs, Dad," Pierre said, his voice uneasy.

"I've got an extra pair here somewhere." Claude sat up, dug into the various pockets of his vest jacket and proffered a couple of loose plugs.

"Gross! Not a pair you've used. I'd rather go deaf."

Bingo. *Fussy. That* was the word. A thoroughly suitable substitute for *quirky*, which Celine couldn't possibly argue with because of empirical evidence. His mood lifted a notch and he cast the plugs in Pierre's direction. They bounced off the boy's chest and whirligigged to the ground. A wounded look spread across Pierre's face, as if the plugs themselves were an insult. Claude shuddered from the futile charade of the entire morning. He wasn't acing parenting and had little juice left by week's end after working sixty hours' worth of numbing labor at the March, so who could blame him? But at that moment he ached for the chance to truly influence his boy—to school him about guns and why they weren't as bad as everyone in the country believed. To convince him to love this fifteen hundred acres that had been handed down through four generations of French-Canadian relations. These notions were as real to Claude as words in a book were to his son.

He grabbed Pierre by the arm and dragged him to a nearby flattened knoll on their property. Looking west and past the Hump, he saw tips of the White Mountains in New Hampshire poking through low clouds. A merlin falcon soared overhead, floating without so much as a single flap. Claude pointed to the sky, and together they tracked the diving raptor, its shrill call resounding as it disappeared, presumably to a nest with young. He was about to mention that the falcon had few predators, but Pierre was busy scribbling something on a tiny pad of paper with a pencil not much bigger, biting his lower lip with concentration.

"That again?" Claude asked, unable to hide his irritation.

"Just some notes," Pierre said, turning his back to Claude.

"What about? The rules of hunting? Put that stuff away. *Merde*."

"Dad! You said you'd leave me alone about my papers. And I know what that word means," Pierre said, aiming his voice at the sky as if wanting the whole world to witness his father's transgressions.

"I guess I did," Claude conceded. "But writing notes isn't going to help your memory."

"How do you know?"

"Well, has there been any improvement?"

"No," Pierre admitted after several seconds, his shoulders slumping in defeat.

"Son, relax. Anyway, you don't need to remember anything about today. So what's the point of writing anything down?"

Pierre shoved the pencil and paper into a shirt pocket. He then pulled out his cell phone and took several shots in all directions. *Click, click, click, click.* With a look of satisfaction that he'd managed to finish what he started despite his father's objections, Pierre then gingerly withdrew two bullets and handed them to Claude.

"Gimme your rifle," Claude said, rolling the bullets around in his palm. Pierre grabbed the firearm from the ground and handed it over like it might explode on its own terms. Claude quickly loaded the rifle, engaged the safety, then handed it back. Pierre, clearly nervous as to what was expected of him, ended up holding the weapon in exactly the wrong direction: straight at Claude's chest.

"Jesus! Get that thing down. What are you trying to do, kill me?"

"Sorry. It's too pointy. And creepy," Pierre said, drawing the rifle away from his father's heart.

"Everything new is creepy at first," Claude said.

"Is that true?" Pierre eyed Claude with suspicion.

"Absolutely."

Pierre gave his father a frightened look for what the future might hold—more factoids of nature to unravel and then endure. Then he began to quiver as he tried to hold back any sound of crying. Claude almost admired him for the effort. He pulled Pierre close and thumbed the tears that had managed to escape. Cupping the boy's chin with his hand, Claude met Pierre's eyes with a smile.

"Come on. Get yourself together. I know things have been rough. But lookit there." Claude pointed east to the farthest horizon. "What do you see?"

"Mrs. Kimbrough's land?" Pierre croaked.

"Christ almighty. Use your imagination for once, will ya? What's in the *far* distance?" Claude didn't wait for an answer. "The Atlantic Ocean."

"I don't see any water, Dad."

"It's not a *literal* question," Claude spat. Though he was momentarily pleased that he himself had landed upon something allegorical—or was it a metaphor? Whatever.

But Pierre was spot-on. They were looking at Kimbroughs' land, alright. Ill-gotten, by Claude's measure. Kimbrough had hijacked the thousand-plus adjacent acres at an estate auction. The previous owners had died suddenly, and pesky lawyers from another part of Maine altogether handled the sale without alerting anyone in Oslo, precluding what would have normally transpired: the townspeople in general, and Claude Roy *specifically*, would've had an opportunity to pull financing together. Though it wasn't exactly their fault, Jim and Sandra Kimbrough had, in essence, swindled Claude out of his right as a born-and-bred Mainer to increase his land holdings. No matter that over the last twenty years the two families had looked out for each other through countless difficult winters, because that's just what people in Maine did. And no matter that Kimbrough had been a decent, and if he was truly honest, bordering on great neighbor. Toss all that aside, he'd never forgiven them and he sure as hell didn't trust them. They were from away. Always would be.

"Dad, when you say literal, do you mean literature? Like my books?" Pierre finally countered, with no small amount of confusion in his voice.

"Forget it," Claude said with resignation. The boy shrugged, clearly happy to reach détente, which left Claude to submerge deeper into a bad itch of late: Sandra Kimbrough.

The day that woman clawed her way into their lives was the day Claude reckoned he'd lost his boy. Not a week after Pierre's accident, Sandra Kimbrough convinced Celine to allow her to teach Pierre the violin. Got her to swallow some guff about how learning an instrument would be good for him, maybe help him with his memory loss. She set Pierre up with a violin so fast, Claude hadn't the time to put a stop to her uppity notions. But damned if Pierre didn't take to the instrument. And it seemed he had a *great ear*, whatever that meant. Claude, on the other hand, was tone deaf—an affliction widely broadcast by Sandra as soon as she'd diagnosed it. Regardless, Claude feared what was next. Macramé? Potting? Sock darning? Pierre would probably be brilliant at that stuff too. But the boy clearly revered Sandra, and Celine had found a new ally and possible best friend. And according to everyone in Oslo, Saint Sandra Kimbrough was just so, so, *so* nice. To Claude's mind, she was a snoopy, crafty little something or other.

"Dad, can we get this over with? I need to get back and practice for my lesson tomorrow."

My God, he couldn't even *think* about that woman without her apparition appearing.

"Mrs. Kimbrough can wait. But I'm curious. Why is it you can remember your violin lesson, but you forgot about our hike this morning?"

"How should I know? I told you. Mostly I can't remember stuff, but sometimes I do. I can't control which. All I know is I need to practice." Pierre sat back down on the rock with a thump.

Claude smeared a crooked/ironic smile on his face, held his hand out—which Pierre grabbed—and pulled the boy back to his feet. They laughed a bit at their choreography and then began to hike toward the northern edge of the property. Soon they arrived at a clearing surrounded by white pines, the destination for their morning practice session. Pierre yawned and then gave Claude a "do we really have to?" look.

"We're only gonna shoot in the air." Claude poked his finger toward the sun and then into Pierre's chest for emphasis, harder than he meant to. The boy staggered back on his heels.

"Won't people hear the shots? It's not hunting season," Pierre said, rubbing his chest. "Even I know that," he added.

Claude closed his eyes and forced himself to count to five. "We're so far north nobody'll know where the shots are coming from, even if they do hear them. Which they won't. Stop worrying."

"But why are we acting as if we're hunting? Because we're not. Not really—right, Dad?"

"We're acting *as if* because hunting is serious business. Even if we mean to kill nothing. Like today. This is a test run for when we do it for real."

Claude rummaged around in his backpack for two fresh pairs of earplugs from the stash he always kept on hand, both in plastic wrappers. Pierre made a small drama of ripping the package open and jamming the plugs deep into his ears. Then, when Claude next spoke, Pierre screamed, "*What*?!" For a moment, this little comedy sketch made Claude feel connected to his boy. Just as quickly, the giddiness evaporated, because he knew very well what separated them. Claude wanted to have a silly day and do boy-like things. He wanted to take risks and cut corners in every direction and then get away scot-free, doing things like shooting rifles off-season. But all of this potential camaraderie was now in question because his son had been damaged. Claude could not bring himself to fully acknowledge that since his accident, Pierre had turned odd and was interested in things that might as well have come from Mars. Like the violin and his lessons with Sandra Kimbrough, as just one example. And as if to pile it on, the Kimbrough property to the east now appeared as some wonderland worthy of a painter he couldn't name. He knew Sandra Kimbrough was not personally responsible for nature's bounty. But she loomed as omnipotent—over land, over Celine, and over his boy.

Claude beckoned to Pierre, who skipped over with the rifle and nestled against him. "Okay, let's get some shots off." Claude knew the boy's face without seeing it: withered, reluctant.

"Ready?"

"Ready," Pierre said with a sigh.

With Pierre in front of him, Claude crouched down and wrapped his arms around the boy. Then he cupped his own hands over Pierre's, with both their fingers at the trigger location of the rifle. He guided it all around, aiming high and low, right and left, mentally urging the boy to relax. With every movement, he felt Pierre's body—stiff and resistant.

"The safety is *on*, Pierre."

With that simple assurance, the boy seemed to sag in a good way, and they continued making these motions so Pierre would trust the rifle, and Claude. Just as he was about to release the safety and aim into the sky, a large smudge of brown, off in the distance, stopped Claude.

"Dad?" Pierre, for once, seemed eager to proceed.

Claude said nothing, but squeezed the boy's torso hard on either side with his upper arms, a signal to remain quiet. After several seconds the smudge began to move, and Claude knew he'd have this thing. He leaned down and whispered, "Hold still, boy. Looks like we got one."

THE MOOSE HAD recovered physically from her ordeal. Lacerations at her throat soon healed, thin scarring now the only outward evidence. General trauma, though, produced stressor hormones in her milk, and this had diminished her calf. Since his birth a few days after her capture and escape, he'd grown at a slower rate and could not seem to fill out. Yet in spite of his scrawny build, the calf tested his muscles and dexterity by scampering about and jumping over downed tree limbs, never wandering far from her smell or calls.

Now in the woods farther north, the moose and her calf roamed among and around thick trees as she searched for food suitable to bolster her newborn. Rounding a bend, she came upon an exposed land depression with a clump of desirable trees in the center. The moose fed on branches, stripping the greenery in one motion and gnashing them with her back molars. Her calf ran up to nurse, and she stopped to allow his head to come in between her hindquarters. He sucked hard for several minutes and then went still. It was as if his month-old instincts were now sharper than hers. Perhaps her vigilance no longer served her. Because what could the moose do but relent when the unnatural world presented her with an experience like that place of death? So it was only when her calf backed away from her udder that she raised her head high. And only then did she see the patch of orange.

THOUGH CLAUDE DIRECTED every inch of movement, they aimed the rifle in tandem toward the brown smudge. Then he carefully released the safety.

"Squeeze it, boy," he ordered in a soft voice.

Pierre froze.

"I said squeeze," Claude whispered tersely.

"It's illegal, Dad."

The boy's voice took on a whiney tone with some amount of defiance. This meant very little to Claude. Not while he was hunting. When it came to animals, he would demand a lot from his son. Trust, of course. Bravery would be a wonderful bonus. But it was important for Pierre to understand that this was a collusion. Like a business deal that, though a gamble, would eventually benefit everyone.

"We're gonna do this."

Pierre began a louder protest, but the sound of his voice was obliterated by the blast Claude forced by squeezing Pierre's finger against the trigger.

ONE DISCHARGE RANG out. The calf's front legs flew out from under his small body while his back legs remained rigid and straight, causing his rump to protrude in the air. His head landed hard on a rock, causing his neck to take on an unnatural slant. Red gushed from his mouth and spewed across a thin patch of snow, the contrast in color stark. Within a few seconds, his back end shivered and collapsed. He lay on his side, eyes open, tongue extended past his lips, which curled up as if in a snarl. Blood, mixed with milk, continued to express from his mouth and saturate the ground. The moose felt all her energy wither as she watched her calf negotiate the shock of his wound with useless writhing. She pushed her snout into his midsection. He rolled in one direction, then immediately lolled back. She observed his skin twitching but knew death was near. She took to a full gallop from a standing position.

CLAUDE COULDN'T BELIEVE he'd missed the thing. The animal, and at this distance it looked to be a large deer, took off at a speed he'd never get used to—probably thirty miles an hour or so. In spite of knowing he didn't have a chance in hell of hitting it, he began, on instinct, to reload. Anyway, it was good for Pierre to see what hunters did, what steps to take. Never give up on the animal. That was a hunter's implicit responsibility. His hands shook as he pulled more bullets out of his vest pocket. That's when he noticed the boy sprawled on the ground, pointing toward Kimbroughs' land.

"I see red!" Pierre yelled, with one hand covering his left ear, the pain of the blast obviously intense despite the plugs.

"Nope." Claude shrugged, shaking his head.

"You hit something, Dad."

"It took off," Claude insisted.

"That's *red*!" Pierre rose to his knees and extended both arms, pointing as if he were shooting. The boy's hunter stance struck Claude as ironic, and he almost chuckled.

But there *was* red. Looking across his land from higher ground into Kimbroughs', Claude saw the bright liquid spreading. He completed reloading knowing that whatever it was, he'd have to put it down. Claude pulled Pierre up by his hand and together they raced down the slope. About two hundred feet from the animal, Pierre broke ahead. He squatted down by its head and placed his hands on the rib cage.

"It's a baby," Pierre said, looking back and testing a smile.

Claude knew that Pierre imagined they could somehow save it from death. He set the gun in the crook of his arm. "Move away from it, boy. It could be diseased," Claude advised quietly.

"We can nurse it, Dad. I know we can," Pierre reasoned with the naïvety of a child promising to take a new puppy out like clockwork four times a day, having no clue as to the commitment. He repositioned himself behind the animal to avoid the blood that continued to drain from its mouth. Then he reached over and covered the animal's eyes with his hands to protect it from seeing its own fate. The calf shifted its head about an inch, an involuntary motion, Claude knew. But now Pierre began to stroke the animal's flank as if encouraging it to wake up.

"You're making it worse. Move away from it, Pierre," Claude said calmly.

Pierre scooted back a few feet. "No gun. *Please*, Dad."

"Okay, son." Claude set the safety into position and placed the rifle behind him. Pierre snuffed back tears, smiling broadly toward the sky as if he couldn't believe his good fortune.

Now Claude knelt to inspect the animal. A cloud of white mucus had moved over its eyeballs, still open but vacuous. The fur was slick with wet and had begun to steam up from the differential in temperature, inside and out. Claude winced; the animal had just involuntarily evacuated its last meal and the odor floated around them. And yet blood continued to flow from the bullet wound. These concurrences of bodily functions were perplexing, and Claude was momentarily mesmerized. Though he had caused this, he felt in awe of the rituals of the body as it moved toward death.

Killing a deer wouldn't have been a catastrophe, even off-season. It happened more often than not, and if the opportunity knocked, local wisdom held that you might as well answer that door. But Claude now grunted with discomfort because this was a moose calf, and that was about as bad as it got. It was something no Mainer, including Claude, would ever consider, if only to ensure future hunting seasons. Beyond that cynical reasoning, a moose calf was sacred in a population that continuously dwindled due to all manner of challenges. Looking at the calf now, Claude saw that it was no bigger than a very large dog. Its flank was gaunt, with ribs protruding and weirdly separated. Claude took hold of the calf's hoof and gently flipped the animal over. The bullet had entered its neck on the other side. He dragged his hand across the body and pressed hard onto the flesh to make sure it was truly dead.

"It's gone. Lucky we didn't need the gun. But we've got to get it on our land," Claude said, worried about potential blowback if Kimbrough discovered what he'd done.

"Why?" Pierre asked.

"You want the front legs or the back?" Claude said, ignoring his question.

Pierre only shrugged.

"What's it weigh? A hundred pounds or so? Not even. Between the two of us we can handle it," Claude said, smiling to encourage Pierre.

Together they picked up the carcass by the hoofs and trudged back up the slope. The thing slung like a hammock, its body flattening the grasses with blood dribbling behind like a trail of liquid crumbs. Claude directed them to a cluster of trees, surely recognizable for when he'd later make arrangements to deal with the body. They lay the animal down and piled dirt and leaves on top.

"Are you *sure* it's dead?"

"It's dead," Claude assured him, nodding gravely.

"You'll bury it?"

"Tomorrow, most likely."

"I want a picture." Pierre already had his phone out, aiming at the dead animal.

Claude quickly grabbed the phone from Pierre and pulled the boy to him. "Why don't we take a selfie instead?" he suggested.

Pierre fit perfectly into the crook of his body, and Claude stretched his arm out to take the shot. They both inspected the picture, which appeared as a typical memento of a father-and-son outing on a Saturday morning in the Maine woods. Then Pierre pulled out the slip of paper he'd secreted in his shirt pocket just an hour before and jotted a few more words.

"Oh, no. Gimme that," Claude said, trying to pluck it from Pierre.

"It's private," Pierre protested weakly, but allowed his father to look at what he'd written on the paper.

First:

Falcon call

44.25 - 70.50

5-29-19

Then:

Rifle shot

THE ACCOMMODATIONS

SANDRA LET HERSELF INTO THE ROY HOME through the back door, which was always unlocked—a Maine custom. As she made her way through the mudroom, she could hear Pierre in his bedroom at the far end of the house attempting to tune his violin, not an easy feat for a young boy. She stopped to listen as he twisted the pegs back and forth until perfect fourth intervals slid into place. Sandra smiled and shook her head with amazement. After just a few weeks, he was getting the hang of it and all she could think was—*wow*. No doubt, the kid had it.

She saddled her purse straps over a wooden wall peg and turned to find Celine at the kitchen table with a cup of tea steeping in front of her. Close-cropped strawberry blonde hair mashed at odd angles from bed head framed Celine's oval face and large green eyes. She was a small woman with no discernable bones, wonderfully smooth and round. Even her knuckles, as she lifted the cup to take a sip, hid under adult baby fat. Sandra, about as thin and boney as could be imagined, envied Celine's apparent ability to feel comfortable with her plump beauty. She was without pretense and thoroughly likable, Sandra had found. Though it had taken them years—and more recently through Pierre's travails—for the women to locate ease with one another.

Sandra helped herself to a cup of hot water from a copper kettle, threw in a lemon wedge, and cocked her hip at the counter. Celine trained a sly smile her way.

"What's up?" Sandra asked.

"Claude's working an extra shift today," Celine announced with satisfaction. The idea of his absence made both women snicker, as if a prank were about to be played.

"It's Sunday. What's that . . . time and a half?" Sandra mused.

Celine rubbed her thumb and forefinger together in the money gesture. "Yeah. And I have the whole day to myself . . . till three, anyway. I should clean the house, but I feel like going back to bed," she admitted, stretching her arms toward the ceiling while yawning.

Sandra noticed her white nightgown was badly yellowed under the armpits. Their eyes met and Celine, embarrassed, drew down her arms and pulled the teacup toward her. She lowered her head to meet the cup halfway, then tipped it to her mouth and took several gulps in a row.

"Why don't you grab a nap? I'll be with Pierre for the next hour," Sandra suggested.

Celine nodded and palmed her lips of moisture, fingers jittering in front of her eyes, then released a sigh, as if even that effort drained her.

Sandra dragged out a chair and sat opposite Celine, whose face glistened with sweat despite a chill in the room. She reached over, took her neighbor's hands and squeezed. Bolstered by this quiet kinship growing between them, Celine had gradually revealed to Sandra the difficulties Pierre was facing due to his memory loss. To a public Oslo, Pierre appeared as affable as ever. But at home, Celine confessed she didn't recognize her son anymore. Pierre used to find amusement in everything.

His cockeyed irony, hilarious. Now he'd stopped smiling, almost as if the muscles around his mouth were disabled. The one and *only* bright spot that had made a dent in Pierre's otherwise gloomy disposition had been learning the violin. And now that Celine was fully onboard with Sandra, the women had begun a persistent campaign to back off Claude. He was the third rail, like an unpredictable electrical spark, who refused to believe that music could ever influence his son for the positive, or even admit to Pierre's considerable talent. As Sandra examined Celine's tired eyes, she couldn't help but wonder how, or even why, the Roys' marriage remained intact.

Celine plucked a small white pill from beneath the saucer and tongued it down. "I'm gonna take a nap. A short one . . . I promise. But if I'm still asleep, wake me when you're finished with Pierre?"

"Sure."

Sandra grabbed a dirty sponge from the sink and was wiping some milk stains off the kitchen table when Pierre came barreling down the hall toward the kitchen. He stuck his head around the corner, violin in hand.

"I got it. I think," he said, waving his bow at Sandra.

"Got what?" Sandra asked, rinsing her hands of sour smell.

"My bow arm!" Pierre sputtered, as if it were obvious.

"We'll see about that," Sandra said with a chuckle, though she had little doubt that whatever Pierre set his mind to, he'd accomplish.

Celine had already dragged her arms onto the table and settled her head. She began to snore her way into a pill-induced nap. Sandra quickly guided Pierre out of the kitchen. As she walked behind him, he swung his violin precariously low to the floor, back and forth as if sweeping leaves from their path. Sandra tapped Pierre on his head.

"Cut it out. Violins will bite if you don't treat them with respect, you know."

He propped the instrument on his shoulder like a baseball bat.

"This okay?" he asked.

"It'll do."

A long hallway connected the kitchen to the rest of the house. The scuffed walls were bare save for two photographs hanging exactly opposite each other. One was a wedding shot of Celine and Claude cutting the cake. They appeared no older than teenagers, with flushed cheeks and uncertain smiles, testing the waters of an adult world. The other was a baby picture of Pierre, perched on the seat of an adult bicycle. Celine and Claude stood on either side, propping him up with protective hands. Pierre looked to be about a year old, wearing an adult-sized blue cap stamped with the March logo, his bright-red hair sprouting from beneath. He was bare chested, and his thin legs dangled out of a diaper. Sandra wondered momentarily why they'd stopped with these two photos; the hallway could have displayed many dozens. Well, she didn't believe in that type of sentimental documentation, either. The shine of life's various milestones tended to dull through the years. At least that's what Sandra's experience had been, and perhaps this was so for Celine and Claude as well.

She nudged Pierre forward. "C'mon, pick up the pace. Jim and I have rehearsal this afternoon."

"*You're* the one who stopped to look," Pierre pointed out.

"True enough," Sandra agreed, laughing.

They proceeded toward a room containing only a few folding chairs placed at random. A single bulb hung from a jerry-rigged wire snaking down about a foot from a jagged hole in the ceiling. At one time this had been the Roy living room. Now it served only as a pass-through space, with five doors leading to other sections of the house.

Over the years and from the distance of their kitchen window, Sandra and Jim had watched with a mixture of fascination and bewilderment as Claude increased the footprint of his house. But she'd only recently gleaned how truly odd the expansion was: impulsive, crude, certainly accidental. Claude had created openings through the living-room walls where it made no sense at all, then slapped together new rooms or even an entire wing. The house had a spooky feel—like a Grimm maze—allowing for no natural intuition as to one's location. As she and Pierre walked toward one of the doors, he playfully tapped the hanging bulb with the back of his violin. It swung in a circle, brushing the garish orange walls with its dim wattage.

When they arrived at Pierre's bedroom, Sandra took out her violin, placing the case at the foot of a utilitarian bunk bed that hugged a long wall. She assumed that at one time the bunks had been intended for sleepovers, though Sandra knew Pierre had a tough time making friends and was especially lonely since his accident. Now the top bed was loaded with books piled flush to the ceiling, and the weight had caused the mattress to sag precariously below. At their first lesson she'd expressed concern that the whole thing might collapse from being top-heavy, or at least, tip over. But Pierre pointed out that he'd wired the bedposts to bolts attached to the structural wall. Claude had been threatening to toss the books out altogether, so Pierre had come up with this solution. His idea actually appealed to Claude, who then helped with the process, and Pierre's precious books were saved from the town dump.

She sat on the bed and plucked her violin strings, which had remained in tune from the previous lessons she'd taught that morning. Pierre stood in the middle of the room, planted his feet apart, and tucked the three-quarter-size violin under his chin. He was small for his age and wouldn't be ready for a full-size instrument for another year at the earliest. But his fingers had a good amount of meat at the tips, and Sandra had high hopes for the tone Pierre might eventually produce.

"Want to test me?" he asked.

She grabbed a sheet of paper off his night table and a rock the size of a tennis ball they'd selected from the driveway. Pierre extended his right arm and then bent it to a little less than forty-five degrees. She then placed the paper on the crook of his elbow with the rock on top, heavy enough to keep the paper in place. Pierre bowed very slowly on the D-string, back and forth, to demonstrate how facile he'd become at maintaining a steady bow stroke while also producing a healthy tone. All the while the paper edges fluttered, but the rock never dislodged from his elbow.

"Am I okay?" he asked as he played.

"Looking good. Sounding good," she murmured with approval.

Now he drew the bow across the other three strings, which caused the rock and paper to tumble to the floor. He broke into a simple melody she'd assigned as part of his lesson. Sandra joined him, providing harmony. Pierre's intonation proved to be almost flawless. If the pitch did veer, it was only because as a beginner he'd not yet mastered any technique to speak of. Still, Pierre heard the problem and adjusted immediately, his intuition uncanny.

In this spartan room, as she corrected his mistakes and reinforced his improvements, Sandra thought about the one thing she meant to incubate in Pierre. Potential. The idea that what was dreamed of in one moment could become a future the next. And it felt almost sacred. If not sacred, then pure. Because she didn't really care if Pierre became a professional violinist. What mattered was that through learning the violin he'd understand that music itself, in whatever form and for the rest of his life, would never fail him. Sandra had not entertained this notion, which she knew to be true for herself as well, for quite some time. When teaching the violin, Sandra had discovered she felt more herself than in all her years as a performer.

At the end of the lesson they packed up their instruments in tandem, like comrades. Pierre opened the double doors to his closet and stowed his instrument on a top shelf. That's when Sandra saw the most astonishing thing. The inside surfaces of both doors were covered, top to bottom, with small pieces of paper a few square inches in size, stapled directly into the wood. The bottom edges had curled up, giving the impression of feathers. Pierre turned and stood between the open doors, watching her reaction.

"What on *earth*?" Sandra declared, looking at him with wonder.

"What do you mean?" Pierre asked, much too innocently.

"All these little papers. What's this about, Pierre?"

"Oh. Just my life," he said nonchalantly while examining his fingernails. The kid was quite the actor when he wanted to misdirect.

"Can I look?" she asked.

"If you want. But they won't mean anything to you."

Sandra gently fingered the papers, noticing some were layered three-deep. The display had been precisely organized with the staples exactly parallel to the top of the paper, and every square was positioned with a one-inch margin on all sides. Great care had gone into this cataloguing, or whatever it was. And Pierre was right—none of it made sense. A few words, a series of numbers, maybe a date. All a kind of coding and penned with perfect lettering:

Rain and thunder
44.05 - 70.71
5-12-19

Mom cried
44.08 - 70.84
5-20-19

Boys laughed
44.01 - 70.23
5-22-19

As she spent a minute scanning the perplexing papers, Sandra wondered if this had something to do with his memory loss. Suddenly, she knew it was true, like an empirical fact of nature, such as birds fly and dogs don't. And now Sandra understood that Pierre *wanted* her to see this, because thinking back over their lessons, she realized he had never opened the closet doors before. But this time he had done so with intention, almost ceremonially. He wasn't testing her, not exactly. More like he wanted to trust her. She felt Pierre watching her as she continued to flip through the papers. He tracked her movements, leaning closer at times to see which paper she'd chosen to read. Every now and again, he'd nod with approval at her choice, though she still couldn't decipher what it all meant.

Then, a loud thump just outside the bedroom, like a piece of furniture tipping over, startled them both. Afraid of what she might find, Sandra grabbed the scruff of Pierre's shirt to hold him back from racing to the door. She opened it a crack and peered out. Celine sat slumped on the floor with her back pressing against the other side of the door. Sandra had no choice but to let it swing open, and Celine collapsed into the room. She lay on her back, still in her nightgown. Sandra was embarrassed that the garment had ridden up almost to Celine's crotch, exposing faint bruises dotting her thighs as if she'd repeatedly stumbled against the same table edge. Then she saw that Celine wore no underwear, and Sandra quickly knelt and tugged the nightgown down. Meanwhile, Pierre had jumped to his mother's head and begun to whisper in her ear. Celine croaked a few words.

"She wants to go to her bedroom," he whispered.

"Can she even walk? How're we supposed to lift her?"

Pierre ignored her questions, and without explanation took over with an expertise that broke Sandra's heart. He crouched over on his hands and knees. Celine used his back as a brace, gathered herself up, and staggered to her feet. Once standing, she leaned against the wall as Pierre positioned himself into her armpit. They clamped their arms around each other's shoulders and waists and began down the hall. Sandra walked alongside, spotting as they hesitated or when Celine teetered toward the wall. Pierre directed them toward a new wing of the house Sandra had not been into.

"This way?" Sandra asked, confused, because she knew the master bedroom was in the other direction.

"Mom's got her own bedroom now. And it'd help if you walked behind us, Mrs. Kimbrough. Sorry, but it'll go faster that way."

Of course. He'd obviously done this for his mother numerous times and suddenly Sandra felt foolish, because what did she really understand about this family?

When they reached the new bedroom, Sandra stood back as Celine accepted the single bed with an odd laugh and curled herself into a ball. Pierre gathered up the bedclothes and swaddled his mother tightly, tucking the sheets under the mattress on one side and placing pillows as a baffle on the opposite. Sandra assumed this was meant to prevent her from falling out of bed. That Celine was now immobilized came as a relief and Sandra released her fists, realizing she'd been clenching them the whole time.

She now looked around what appeared to be the largest room in the house, certainly enormous for a bedroom by typical Maine standards. The walls had been primed, and a few different samples of pink/peach color had been patched here and there for selection. A single chest of drawers was clearly inadequate to accommodate the multiple piles of clothing lying on much of the floor. Then, Sandra turned around to discover what could only be described as a circus spectacular. A couple dozen pairs of high-end shoes were displayed on a shelf spanning the wall width. Curious, she walked over and examined the labels: Louboutin, Blahnik,

Choo, Kors, to name a few that Sandra recognized. All with four-inch heels, minimum. Each posed in proud profile, almost brazen. Treasured objects, to be sure. And very expensive.

Sandra glanced at her watch and felt a small panic. "Lord. I've got to run, Pierre. You know what to practice for next week?"

"D major and minor scales. The next two pages of the melody book?"

"Right."

"Can I do another scale? Maybe A."

"I'll leave that for you to decide."

He nodded yet looked uncertain about her meaning.

"Don't move forward with A until the D scales are correct," she explained.

Sandra left the Roy house fascinated by Pierre's secret papers, baffled by Celine's impressive footwear, but also disturbed by her friend's apparent use of pills. Witnessing the complex layers of the Roy family revealed not clarity, but rather a thick confusion. But that was Maine. Certainly Oslo. And as she drove the short distance up the hill to her house, another thought came to mind. The Roys' sex life was at a standstill, probably had been for some time. Sandra wondered why this was even interesting. But it was.

She crested the hill and when her house came into view, she spied Jim spread-eagled across the solar panels that blanketed their roof. The electric bill had come in a good bit higher over the last months, and they suspected that one or more of the connections had been damaged during the unusually inclement winter they'd recently endured. Jim insisted they avoid a costly service call on the system, which had outlived its warranty by more than ten years. So Sandra was now relieved to see Jim pinwheeled for a look-see.

Although she'd married a guy who could coax almost anything back to life, she squeezed the steering wheel with apprehension. The plans they'd put in place to live partially off the grid had not proved anywhere near successful, mostly because neither of them had a disciplined head for finance. As a result, Sandra had learned to tolerate debt like it was a familiar reaper making monthly appearances; their incomes rarely squared with the bills. Jim must have heard her tires crunch over the rough gravel, because he lifted his head and grinned in her general direction. Sandra nodded to herself—perhaps some good news. And she gave in to a smile as well, because oh boy, did she have some great gossip.

Sandra parked her car between Jim's pickup truck and her motorbike at the back of their house. She swung the door open and almost stepped into a six-foot-square puddle of slush. Just when those in Oslo thought it was safe to change out seasonal wardrobes, Maine would famously claw back the winter with a surprise snowfall, which still covered the surrounding dense woods. Now, the late-spring melt had created a steady stream of water feeding directly into their parking area. Sandra dragged rubber boots from the back of the car, tossed her flats onto the passenger seat, and jammed her feet into the clodhoppers. When she stepped out, she sank a few inches into half-frozen water. Undeterred, Sandra jumped over several miniature lakes and reached the house in time to steady the bottom rungs as Jim descended the shuddering ladder.

"You'll never guess what," she baited him.

Jim leapt down from three steps up and pivoted. He grabbed her ponytail at the rubber band, slid his hand down her almost-waist-length rope of silver hair, and then wound it back up to her neck as if it were a skein of yarn. Searching her hazel eyes for a few seconds, Jim shook his head and planted a dry kiss on the tip of her nose. Which meant he couldn't fix the panels. Which meant paying for the solar company to come out, and they'd surely advise replacing the whole shebang. Which meant they were, yet again, financially gutted. Dread swarmed much too fast. She bit her lower lip to hold back any show of emotion—anger or tears. Gossip about the Roys' lackluster sex life now seemed trivial.

Sandra pushed Jim's arms away and he let her hair swing free from his fist. She looked him up and down with impatience, an emotion that had quickly supplanted her fear of certain financial ruin because Jim was still in his pajamas. They'd need to leave within the hour if they were to arrive in Portland on time for orchestra rehearsal. She pointed to his plaid flannels with derision and simultaneously began a mental inventory of monies they currently owed. Her gynecologist and his cardiologist. Perimenopause was making her certifiable, and bad tickers were rampant on his side. And their deductibles for both were so high they'd be satisfied only if one of them stroked out and then survived in a lifelong coma. The dentist. Two crowns for him, a root canal for her. Regular cleanings had become a quaint memory. The Oslo grocery store—an awkward situation. The manager, who'd propositioned Sandra when they first moved to Oslo about twenty years earlier, had agreed to hold over a tally that had grown to an embarrassing sum. She recently began shopping two towns over to avoid his expectant gaze. Sandra wasn't sure which he hoped for most, the money or sex. She almost regretted not giving the guy a mercy fuck way back when, before he'd ballooned to three hundred pounds; maybe he'd forgive their current bills. Now the list would include Maine Solar Solutions, whose tagline was "A lifetime of worry-free energy!"

The past year had been even more challenging due to both Jim's cello and her violin needing major overhauls. Their luthier in Boston wouldn't offer them credit, and actually refused to return the repaired instruments until Jim first handed over not a check, but a wad of cash. Jim was insulted by what he saw as a cluttering of his "high art" with the luthier's "low commerce." But with past transactions the man had waited months and months to be paid, so Sandra couldn't exactly blame him for holding their instruments hostage. They'd performed on their much inferior B instruments until the debt was satisfied. Sandra threw these thoughts aside because, really, what was the point? Lack of money had been their ménage-a-trois partner for years.

"Seriously. Guess," Sandra prodded again.

"Can't wait," Jim deadpanned, and leaned back against the ladder with arms crossed.

"It's really good."

"Where's my cello?"

"Already in the truck. Come on, guess!"

"We have to *go*. And I'm starving," he whined.

"Claude and Celine aren't sleeping together."

"Oof." Jim winced.

"Right?"

"Celine tell you?"

"Not exactly . . ."

"Well, this should be interesting. That man is a fuse aching to be lit."

"I know. But let's get some soup. Anyway, it'll take the entire drive to explain."

"Can't wait," Jim repeated, rolling his eyes.

They walked around to the front of their 1840 home. The restored farmhouse was on the Maine historic register but hadn't looked as if it qualified since forever. Jim cared little for any pretense of aesthetic maintenance (not to mention system repairs), and only when there was a dire need at that. Instead, he applied all his elbow grease to working a year-round greenhouse, which they relied on for the greater percentage of their food. All part of that grid business.

As they walked around to the front of the property, Sandra dragged her hand along the dark-grey paint, peeling off like shredded paper, and rubbed the color between her fingers. The flecks disintegrated to dust. She gazed up at the gutters under the roofline. A few drops promptly hit her forehead. They hadn't been cleared of dead leaves from last fall and were now a repository for stagnant water. She wiped the moisture from her brow and took a whiff. Mold, mixed with sour milk from Celine's dirty kitchen table.

Sandra pulled off her muddy boots, propping them against the bottom step for when they'd soon leave for Portland, and nudged open the front door with her toe. They tunneled through the living room, filled with gunmetal shelving units that housed volumes of books and music scores. Decorative oddities peppered the room, such as a collection of splintered rowboat oars that had been bolted to the walls as a kind of folk art. Ceramic and wooden bowls, filled with buttons sorted by every color imaginable, lined the ledges of tall windows along the front of the house. A tricycle standing in as a side table, its seat just wide enough for a single cup of coffee, sat by a sofa whose batting had exploded at various split seams. With so much ongoing scavenging, the living room might have felt overly busy. But a double-height ceiling with a walking loft at one end mitigated that well enough. And because the house sat back from the public road with a quarter-mile drive, curtains weren't necessary. This unrestricted light had allowed Sandra to be adventurous with color. She'd painted the walls a deep lapis blue, which at night appeared almost black, like a gorgeous bruise. Sandra appreciated all this cockeyed beauty and by rescuing what others considered useless, she felt both thrifty and benevolent.

They rounded the corner into the kitchen, all whitewashed cabinets and stainless steel. She headed directly for the fridge and grabbed a container of homemade cucumber soup, then brought bowls down from a shelf above the stove, which she filled with soup and topped with a sprinkle of dill. They stood next to each other, their bodies canted against the butcher-block counter, and slurped the cold meal.

"You'll call the solar company in the morning?" Sandra asked, wiping her mouth with a dishrag.

"I guess."

"Jim, we can't continue to pay electric bills this high," she said, throwing the rag into the sink.

"Summer's coming. We could turn the heat off now. Not call till September. That'll save some money. Wear sweaters at night?" He trotted out his reasoning between gulps.

"*There's* a plan," Sandra said.

She squinted from the early afternoon sun, which had struck her face with surprising intensity, grateful for its warmth in the chilly room. Now that their solar panels were null and void, maybe the mild weather predicted for the next couple of days would not only heat the house, but also dry up some of the mud on their private road. That they'd never paved their driveway in all these years suddenly deflated what little energy she had left after teaching all morning. Shocking, how she'd gotten used to the many indecent ways they continued to live. Sandra should have been resolved by now, but the ongoing indignities reinjured her in strangely cumulative ways. Somewhere in there was the textbook definition of insanity: to hope for different results even as Jim never changed.

Sandra glanced up at Jim's profile as he swallowed the last drops of soup: an Adam's apple that never seemed to stop pumping, a patrician sniffer. He was as skinny as the day she'd met him, with hair still brown like saddle leather and smiling blue eyes with wrinkles in all the right places. Jim's was an indisputably attractive presentation that many people equated with wisdom. He was perceived as a man of lofty principles and reasonable solutions. And all of that was true enough, because Jim *was* the de facto voice of reason in Oslo. Listening to all sides, he never raised his voice while negotiating disputes among neighbors. In short, Jim lent a level head to gnarly small-town conflicts. Yet the platitudes that impressed others did nothing to assuage the fact that they were broke about three hundred sixty days of the year. And privately, Jim was aghast that

Sandra, out of financial desperation, had deigned to start teaching. He claimed it gave the wrong impression and diluted how they were seen as artists, even in a town where that particular nuance rarely registered on anyone's mind other than Jim's.

"Musicians do their work out of love," Jim had declared.

"Who are you talking to? The local dry cleaner? Do you even hear yourself? Musicians have to find ways to *support* themselves, too," she'd counter with a pinched smile, because Jesus, playing in a per-service part-time orchestra in Maine wasn't exactly lucrative.

"Those who can, perform. Those who can't, teach."

"Fine. Tell that to the luthier the next time we need overhauls. I'm sure he'll waive the bill when he finally *understands*."

Sandra didn't enjoy bringing Jim down several notches every few weeks, but he forced her hand with his manifestos from on high. And so, it was with unexpected delight and, if she was honest, abject relief that she'd easily built up a full teaching studio in no time. Sandra traveled to neighboring towns called Norway, Denmark, Mexico, and Peru to teach the odd child who showed even a mild interest at twenty bucks per half hour. For larger families she managed to rope in three or four siblings, each handing one violin off to the next. Oftentimes she threw in the last lesson at no charge as an incentive, or a simple kindness. And it broke her heart to learn that people she had lived among for years were, in fact, desperate for music. They hadn't understood the need until Sandra had satisfied it.

They finished up their soup, and Sandra stacked the dishes into the dishwasher while Jim watched her.

"Why are you standing there? Go get dressed. We're late as it is," Sandra said.

"I don't like you teaching Pierre," he said.

"I know you feel that way, but there's nothing you can do about it.

We need the money."

"It's not a good idea. They're too close to our house. Proximity. Plus, Claude's crazy."

"I'm aware of that, too. But the kid needs me."

"You can't fix that family, Sandra."

"I am *not* the naïve one," she said, slamming the dishwasher closed and punching the start cycle.

"I'll be down in a few minutes," he said, walking out of the kitchen.

"I'll be in the truck."

THE MOOSE KNEW the large metal container provided salt and because it was not in motion, she also understood it to be safe. Approaching, she saw a female human inside who looked to be asleep. This would normally deter the moose, as she'd found many humans to be unpredictable. But once she came closer, the moose recognized this human to be the female with long white fur and an odor of violets, whom the moose had first encountered while searching for a secluded area to birth her calf.

That day, the moose walked into a clearing and spotted a metal container approaching. Preparing to abandon the area, the moose then noticed that this metal container was different; it seemed unusually small, and a female human sat on top. Stopping a fair distance away, the female human shoved a dark patch from her eyes. The air shuddered and the moose sensed her fear, but this human made no motion to approach or make noises. She then directed the metal container in the opposite direction and disappeared. All that remained was the scent of violets. Within the hour, the moose began to birth her calf.

Now the moose licked salt off the large metal container as the female human with long white fur and an odor of violets slept inside.

SANDRA STARTLED AWAKE, out of breath and in a full-body sweat.

She'd been idling the truck with the heat on full blast while waiting for Jim to join her for the drive to Portland. According to the dashboard clock only ten minutes had passed, but she'd succumbed to that bottomless sleep where her orientation was so scrambled that if she woke on the moon it might have made some sense. As she reached over to turn off the ignition, Sandra looked up and saw a large patch of brown in front of her. The brown quivered. Then she realized that this brown was actually twitching fur. The moose saturated the entire windshield. Sandra wiped sweat from her forehead and slunk down in her seat. Seemingly unaware of her presence, the moose swung her head around and began to lick salt from the engine hood. Having tongue-washed a section on the driver side, she shifted to where Sandra sat, and in doing so presented her flank. Sandra noticed old and deep scars incised across the fur, the slashes resembling the intricate cross-hatching work of an imprecise basket weaver. And also what looked like a more recent wound at her neck—healed yet still red. The moose stopped in mid-motion and seemed to look directly at Sandra, then abruptly turned and walked toward the woods, pausing at intervals to emit a grunt call. Sandra looked around, hoping to catch sight of the calf, as well. Oddly, he didn't appear, and the moose was soon swallowed by the dense trees.

Sandra had first seen the calf a few weeks earlier. He looked to be the scrawniest newborn imaginable, and so helpless he seemed tethered to his mother by an invisible leash. If he did dawdle, the moose always, always, waited for him. Or gave him a strong nudge, as if to say, "The world waits for you, until it doesn't." Since then, Sandra had seen them roaming often, either on her land or next door on the Roy property. Just the previous week, Sandra had spotted the moose emerging from the lake with a dripping hunk of greens in her mouth, heading for her calf, who paced the shore, waiting. The two then consumed food—the calf urgently at her udder, the moose masticating the greens in slow motion. One never interfered with the other, even as they ate at divergent paces. Sandra wanted to remember how untainted this mutual accommodation appeared to be.

Sandra could've easily drifted off again, her exhaustion was that deep. But since waking, she couldn't help but think how she knew more about the Roy family dynamics than she probably should. And now Jim's warnings of not getting involved didn't seem such an unreasonable admonition. But really, all that was boilerplate. What Sandra was ashamed to admit was that she envied the shoes. It seemed next to impossible that Claude made enough to afford designer shoes by working the occasional additional shift at the March. But the Jimmy Choos were there, which meant that somehow Claude Roy had extra money. And she felt deprived.

Dragging her ponytail around, Sandra inspected the split ends. She'd neglected to wash her hair or even shower before teaching that morning, because the house was particularly cold. It then occurred to her that Jim had actually turned the heat off the previous night, which had been one of the suggestions he'd trotted out earlier as a way to cope without fixing the solar panels till September. And now that the house had warmed up, he was delaying their trip to Portland by indulging himself with a shower. In evidence were beads of water dribbling down the upstairs window by the claw-foot tub, creating vertical tracks in the steam. She rolled down the truck window.

"Get out of that shower!" she screamed at the top of her lungs.

A few crows flew for cover. Jim acknowledged by rubbing the window clear of fog and giving her a thumbs-up. Sandra felt re-chilled and turned the ignition on again for more heat.

During the upcoming drive she'd not talk about Celine's pills, or her expensive fuck-me shoes on display in her new private bedroom. She wouldn't even broach the gossip she'd dangled earlier about their neighbors' sex life. She'd keep Pierre's secrets about tiny papers and cryptic words and coded numbers. And she'd hold back her revelation that teaching violin was about the best thing that had ever happened to her. Rather, she'd listen, again, to Jim's rationale for turning off the hot water heater at night. She wouldn't nail him that she knew he'd already done it. They'd agree to wait. Maybe trade off showers every other day. She'd wear the same clothes three days in a row. They'd do many things like this and a lifetime of marital accommodations would continue to build upon itself. Meanwhile, Jim would continue to try and fix the solar panels. The air blew hard and hot from the truck vents. Sandra could smell her own sweat, which ran like oil off her skin. They'd now have to break speed limits to make the rehearsal on time. She began to weep.

THE FEMALE HUMAN had begun to make movements, so the moose walked away. Her udders were still full, swaying and uncomfortable. She emitted her grunt calls, now strictly instinct; her calf had died the day before. When she was well hidden among the trees, she looked back to see the female human poke her head from the container and howl. The female then thrashed her head from side to side, causing her long white fur to fly everywhere. Her body trembled. The moose understood these motions to be something other than aggression.

NOTHING HAPPENS BY ACCIDENT

HE STOOD AT THE PERIPHERY OF THE school gymnasium and watched his classmates gather in groups, jumping like jackrabbits and jabbering on about summer plans. They'd just been dismissed from their final seventh-grade assembly on the last day of school. Pierre understood all the commotion, because it was early June and summer had officially launched with two options: camp for those who could afford such extras, or plain old zip for everyone else. Pierre was a member of the zip group. But no matter which fate fell upon what kid, screaming about it seemed to be required. A girl, the frequently mean ringleader in his class, howled like she was about to be thrown off a cliff, a fate Pierre thought most days she deserved. The mob matched her howl for howl, and within seconds the entire space throbbed.

Since his brain had gone haywire, Pierre experienced loud sounds and high pitches as unbearable. And though he had no control over in-voluntary spazzes when the noise went beyond his tolerance—like his hands flying to his head and his fingers diving deep into his ears, or his body going stiff and then quivering from shoulders to knees—this time,

Pierre wrapped his arms around his middle and tried very hard not to go all dorky. It didn't work. The Ringleader pointed at him and announced to her awful friends that he reminded her of a zombie. Since he didn't want to be labeled anybody's walking dead, and as a final desperate act, Pierre decided to follow the brain doctor's advice. The *nothing* exercise.

Closing his eyes, he relaxed his shoulders, shook out his hands, counted to ten and thought of . . . *nothing*. At the exact moment of . . . *nothing*, everyone in the gym roared like a flash mob, instantly causing his heart to pound. Just as quickly, his fingers twitched and his legs went rubbery. Pierre squeezed his eyes shut and imagined he was on another planet, because he actually *felt* like a zombie. And . . . *nothing* turned out to be about the stupidest advice he'd ever received.

Keep repeating the exercise until it works.

Things don't get better overnight.

Be patient . . .

Those were the exact words his doctor had used to encourage him a few weeks earlier, when Pierre had described *nothing* as one hundred percent, totally lame. Shoulder-relaxing, hand-shaking, and counting numbers was easy enough—any drip could get those down. But . . . *nothing*? How was that possible? Even his mom had to muffle a laugh when the doctor continued to blather on forever about . . . *nothing*.

Nothing seems like a difficult concept.

But it's really quite simple.

Just empty your mind . . .

This was how the doctor had further explained his so-called theory at the next office visit, which happened to be the one and only time Pierre's dad ever attended. "Really? *That's* the best ya got?" his dad yelled on his way out the door. Pierre couldn't blame him and only wished he could walk out, too.

Actually, between appointments, Pierre had been giving the brain doctor's theory of *nothing* some thought. The guy had gotten it totally backward, and Pierre couldn't wait to correct him. He'd explain that there was no such thing as *nothing*—there was only *everything*. Big bang whatever, quantum yadda, quark blah blah. And the *theory of everything,* which at the moment Pierre knew pretty much nothing about. But he must have read about it at some point, because he'd thought of it. Plus, it sounded cool. And huge geeks like Einstein and Stephen Hawking understood this stuff. Useless nothing doctor.

Now he was thinking very hard and feeling way too much, which made Pierre's vision go kind of wavy. The floor surged up and he felt on the verge of collapsing. But fainting in front of the Ringleader was not a possibility; he saw her circling him, ready to pounce with her snark. She was really pretty and too thin. (All the mean ones were.) Pierre willed his head to clear, and more importantly, not to cry.

"Stupid brain trauma. Stupid brain trauma. Stupid brain trauma," he repeated softly to himself, which was as close to *nothing* as he could summon.

Quiet. Quiet. Quiet. He tried that too, but more as a simple wish that it might come true.

The world is a noisy place.

We can't control things.

You will get through this . . .

His doctor had made him this promise on Pierre's most recent visit. Adding to these assurances, the doctor crossed his heart hoping to die, and even swore on his mother's grave. What a phony. Pierre's mom and dad promised stuff to each other all day long by swearing on their parents' graves, and both sets of grandparents were still alive. That's when Pierre quit trusting his doctor.

The gym was now almost empty. Just a few kids, including Pierre, were waiting for parents to collect them. Thanks to the relative quiet, his heartbeat slowed. The sweat on his palms finally dried and he held out one hand to test the tremors—his fingers stiff as pencils. For a moment Pierre considered the possibility that the *nothing (*or was it the *quiet?)* exercise had worked, but then immediately dismissed that idea because simple logic told him otherwise. When the kids left the gym, the screeching stopped. That's when he felt better. It was an example of cause and effect, which was an *actual* theory. Not some *nothing* foolishness. Idiot doctor.

Pierre leaned against the cement wall, grateful for its cool surface. He canted one leg in front of the other, another attempt to appear normal for the Ringleader, who'd just smiled at him. She'd tried this before—a trick to make him smile back. But as soon as he did, she'd turn around and walk away. Now, Pierre thwarted her by turning away first. This felt like a victory for about five seconds. Then doubt set in, because Pierre had no clue what the Ringleader actually meant to him, other than being a victim of her evil methods of torture. This was what his life had become. He'd lost huge blocks of time. Then he'd suddenly remember small chunks, which felt like his brain had somehow decided to be nice and give him a break. But those pieces, however arranged, rarely seemed to make much sense. Now, the Ringleader got distracted by her creepy friends and left the gym. Pierre breathed deeply, pulled out his phone, and tapped the photo icon to review the four pictures he'd taken the day before.

The images were the flip side of his papers. He'd look at them, say, a week later, and hopefully remember what had happened. Initially, studying them brought back almost nothing. And on rare occasions an image would produce a vague recollection, though he couldn't seem to build on it for any concrete meaning. But over the past weeks Pierre had discovered something amazing: sound was the hook into his memory. By taking pictures where he could connect what he'd *heard* to the event, Pierre had begun to reconstruct his life.

Image 1. The long stretch on Crescent Road—a bunch of

noisy crows.

Image 2. A dirt path along the lake—two dogs had snarled at each other.

Image 3. The Wilsons' chicken coop—mean kids had laughed at him.

Image 4. That steep hill on Wickham Avenue—a truck had screeched to a stop.

He slid down the wall, propped his rear end on the heels of his sneakers, and got to work. Of the four sounds from the previous day's pictures, Pierre thought the crows might be important. It was a deduction of pure instinct; crows seemed like happy birds and at the moment, Pierre ached for something, *anything*, happy. He finger-dragged the image into the latitude-longitude app. Once identifying the coordinates, he searched them in Google Earth. Tweezing his fingers apart on the screen, he zoomed in and began examining the image to figure out why the crows were connected to the straightaway on Crescent Road and, more importantly, why he'd snapped the photo in the first place. What had happened?

For a few minutes he moved the picture right and left, up and down. He saw the road and trees and a fence, and even a house in the distance. The clouds in the sky looked to be mare's tails, which his dad said meant rain the next day. Not one memory broke through. He looked around the gym and saw that he was now completely alone. This was hard work, and Pierre's head began to pound. A terrible sense of doom came over him, a hopelessness that things would never get better. Which made him think of his mom, who asked him endlessly what had happened the day of his accident. And his dad, who never, ever mentioned it. And that made them both, in different ways, sad. And because he still couldn't remember a thing about that day, Pierre *knew* he was the cause of everyone's unhappiness.

Then, a memory.

They were in the car on their way back home from getting ice-cream cones. Pierre's mom was crying, which was normal these days. His dad drove with both hands on the steering wheel, something he didn't often do. But he'd just thrown his barely eaten cone out the window because he was angry with Pierre's mom, which was why he was two-fisting it. Pierre sat in the backseat watching their heads bob from the pitted road as his parents argued about stuff he didn't want to hear. He stuck the last of his cone into his mouth, wiped his hands on his khaki pants, and slipped his fingers into his ears. Then his mom grabbed his dad's arm and the truck swerved badly to the right, causing them to pull to the side of the road. His dad turned off the engine. Pierre needed to pee and hoped the fight wouldn't last too long.

They got stuck on small things that bugged his dad. Like why was the house so filthy and why wasn't there any milk in the refrigerator and the fact that he couldn't find a clean pair of underwear. And how he worked like a mule to provide for them and how he had the equivalent of a two-by-four's worth of dust in his lungs to prove it. And that he was at his *limit*.

And then her usual defense. Like she'd washed a few dishes that very morning and she'd planned on shopping later in the day and why didn't he just do his own laundry for once in his life. And that she worked hard raising their son. And that his lungs were fine. And how she was doing her best and that he asked too much of her. And that she felt so *sad*.

His dad was quiet for a few seconds and Pierre thought they might be finished.

But, then.

Like how her breath was bad and her teeth were dirty and how she wasn't even wearing a bra and that she stank to the heavens and she wasn't functioning and that he was only human and *mon Dieu* when was she planning on getting herself *together*.

And then.

Tomorrow. And his dad said *really* and his mom said *yes* and his dad said *you've said that before* and his mom said *this time I mean it* and his dad said *I'll believe it when I see it* and his mom said *it's true* and his dad said *qu'en est-il des fucking pilules* and his mom said *I threw the fucking pills out this morning.*

His dad looked back at him and motioned for him to climb into the front seat. Pierre scrambled onto his lap and his dad said, *Here is your son. Say it to him.* Her lips trembled. She wiped her eyes and used the tears to rub dried ice-cream drips from her chin. She cleared her throat. *No more pills.* She crossed her heart and swore it on the grave of her mother, whom they'd had dinner with the week before. *No. More. Pills.*

The sky suddenly filled with millions of shrieking crows, as if her promise had the effect of a bird bomb. Pierre's heart exploded with the love he felt for her and his need for her to return to the way she used to be. How she'd check his homework, though it wasn't necessary. And fix every meal, she was such a good cook. And let him read passages of books to her, even though her thing was celebrity magazines. And tell him what clothes matched, because he was slightly color-blind. And his dad stroked his mom's cheek, the way he used to show her affection. And she smiled at him through tears, but the good kind. And Pierre believed, deeply, deeply, deeply, that she had, in fact, flushed the *pilules* down the toilet. And they hugged each other and cried and cried and cried. And then Pierre remembered that after they'd finished crying, and after the crows had flown away, he'd wondered if it was now safe to be happy.

Glancing up at the clock on the wall, Pierre saw he had only five minutes before his mom would arrive to pick him up. He quickly pulled paper and a pencil from his back pocket and made his notes about the memory from the day before.

Crows - Mom No Pills
44.02 - 77.13
6-11-19

He stood up and tucked it into his breast pocket, close to his body. The paper, the memory, felt safe. Maybe it was real. He smiled. Then a boy ran up and skidded to a stop.

"Hey, Roy. We're going to Ben's house to play video games. Wanna come? His mom's ordering pizza."

"Thanks, but my mom's picking me up. We've got some stuff to do."

Pierre knew this was a mercy invite. The kid threw him a barely disguised relieved smile and flew off to Ben and pizza and videos. And Ben's mom. Pierre had no idea who these people were.

Out in the parking lot, his mom's car approached at the same time as the Ringleader's mother's. They waved to each other. Pierre walked over to the open window on his mom's side of the car, crossed his arms, and shook his head.

"What's wrong?" she asked.

"Why did you say hi to her?"

"What do you mean? Mrs. Cabot?"

"Why did you wave at her?"

"She's a friend. The waving kind."

"Her daughter is *mean*."

"Which one?"

"The one in my class!" he shouted with exasperation.

"Her name is—" she began.

"No! I don't remember her name and don't tell me."

"Stop it, Pierre," she said with a sigh.

He jumped into the car and saw immediately that his mom was on her pills. She raked her fingers through her hair, and he noticed the filth under her nails. Her hands, slack, slipped around the steering wheel as she pressed on the gas too hard. They jolted forward several feet, then rolled to a stop. Pierre struggled for a sound, anything to hold on to, but the whole world had gone silent. He grabbed his mom's chin, pulled it in his direction, and smiled at her. "Ben asked me to go to his house for pizza," he said, forcing a laugh.

"You knew him? Remembered? Why didn't you go?" she asked, digging around in her purse for tissues. She blew her nose and wiped her forehead, then jammed the tissue under her thigh. The floor of the car was littered with balled-up tissues. He'd need to clear them out before his dad got home. To make sure he remembered, Pierre grabbed one, still moist with her snot, and stuck it in his breast pocket next to the memory paper.

"We talked about later in the week," Pierre lied.

"Good, honey. Sounds like you're making progress."

He nodded once. "Yeah."

"I'll call Ben's mom tomorrow," she promised.

She slipped the car into gear, then pressed on the brake and accelerator simultaneously. The engine drilled. Pierre nudged her leg and pointed to the pedals. Stifling a giggle, she reshuffled her feet while Pierre slunk down and buckled his seat belt.

Once home, she busied herself with the fairy tale of attending to this and that. Pierre's Ben lie floated like a cherry garnish on top; he knew it had soothed her. And as she paced the labyrinth of the house, he watched her more closely than any twelve-year-old should, trailing her with what he thought was appropriate distance. Finally, they landed in the kitchen and Pierre fixed them both a sandwich. She picked at the tuna between slices of white bread and, ignoring the napkin Pierre had laid across her lap, licked her fingers like a movie star.

During the dead times, when her eyes shuttered and her chin drooped to her chest, he snuck in a paragraph or two of *Franny and Zooey*. The head librarian said the book was for adults, like she'd warned about most of the books he wanted to read. But Luc's gram thought he could handle it, and everybody, including his mom and sometimes even his dad, went along with what Mrs. Sibley said. He'd finished the entire chapter by the time his mom excused herself to the bathroom off the long hall. *Be right back*. She always said that. Pierre held his breath as he heard the toilet flush after she peed. The faucet splashed. He imagined the rattle of the bottle. He imagined her pulling out a pill and swallowing it. He knew it was real when she didn't return to the kitchen.

Pierre retreated to his bedroom, feeling oddly flat. He stapled his memory to the inside of the closet door like a dutiful soldier. The still-wet tissue ball bulged at his breast pocket. When he lobbed it against the wall, it skittered under his bed and Pierre knew if he didn't retrieve it right away, he wouldn't remember. Then his dad would see all the tissues in the car and know that his mom had lied yesterday in the car and was still on her *pilules*. His head throbbed from all the many ways he needed to protect her. The pain burrowed between his eyes, then shot up and over and down the back of his neck. He held on to the side of his bed with one hand, the other smothering his mouth. What had the doctor said about pain this bad? Something about a bleed. But Pierre knew the real reason for such pain: his mom and her pills. The ache drove him to his knees, and he lay his torso across the bed, his fingers pulling hard on his hair. Stop. Stop. Stop. Dumb doctor.

He woke to find himself curled in bed with a book he'd never opened before leaning against his chest. The tissue, now dry, was clamped in his fist. Though fatigue still traced every bend of his body, the pain was gone, along with any memory of selecting this book from the top bunk or crawling under the bed to rescue the tissue. Or even pulling a blanket over his body.

A sharp crack in the distance brought Pierre to a sitting position. Not a minute later, he heard Mrs. Kimbrough drive up on her motorbike, whose putt-putt engine he always recognized. Pierre's mood brightened, pleased with the prospect of seeing his teacher on a day other than his lesson. When he rounded the corner, she was already sitting at the kitchen table.

"Where's your mom?" she asked, looking worried.

He stared at the floor, trying to recover the last couple of hours.

"Is she asleep?" she prompted.

"Yeah, I think so. But so was I. We take a lot of naps."

"But you heard the shots?"

"*Something* woke me up. Was it a rifle?"

"Uh-huh. At least I think so," Mrs. Kimbrough said, nodding. "I came over to see if your mom knew anything about it."

She looked around their messy kitchen and began to fill the sink with soapy water and pile in the dishes that littered the kitchen counters. Pierre felt embarrassed.

"You don't have to do that."

"I can't help it," she said, smiling. "Clean surfaces and sudsy sinks make me happy."

While she scraped and washed three days' worth of dried crud off the plates, Pierre wiped them dry. Standing next to her, he grabbed shy glances of his teacher. He assumed she'd been to Portland for orchestra rehearsal that day, because she was dressed differently from her usual jeans and T-shirts. Her grey hair was wrapped in a bun at her neck with a pink scrunchie. He spied the curve of her breasts under her form-fitting white blouse. Poking out of slim black pants with cuffs were brown leather shoes that for some reason had cats drawn on top. Pearls popped off her ears. As usual, she smelled of violets, which used to bug him. Now he counted on her scent because it was one of the few things he always, always remembered, and that was a comfort. He decided Mrs. Kimbrough wasn't exactly pretty—not like the Ringleader—but someone you'd definitely notice in a crowd.

"When do you think your mom might get up?" she asked after she'd finished stacking the dishes into the upper cabinets.

"Maybe kids are playing with BB guns," Pierre suggested, trying to keep his mom out of the conversation.

"Nope, I know the difference. Definitely a rifle."

Just then, another shot rang out.

"This is crazy! I mean, once in a while is fine. People do what they do. But I've been hearing it on and off for the last hour. And much too close to our houses."

Pierre's body stiffened. The shot, the *sound*. He felt a memory surfacing. "I might know something about it," he said quietly.

"How?"

"My papers?" he offered tentatively.

"Show me."

Pierre ran to his room with Mrs. Kimbrough at his heels. He swung the closet doors open and swept his hands over the feathery papers as if touching might speed his search. Then he slowed down and flipped through each paper individually until he found it. He pried the staple out with his fingernails and flattened the paper between his palms. Mrs. Kimbrough had been standing at the door watching him, and Pierre motioned for her to sit on the bed.

"See?" he said, sitting next to her and pointing to the coding. "This is from about a week ago."

Falcon call
44.25 - 70.50
5-29-19
Rifle shot

She shook her head. "This makes absolutely no sense. You're going to have to explain it, Pierre."

His parents saw him take the pictures. But lots of kids did that for social media, which was normal enough. When he wrote down the notes, though, his mom acted like she didn't notice, and his dad tried to get him to stop. But Pierre knew all that was fake. His dad didn't care in the least and his mom was really scared. Mrs. Kimbrough was a different kind of adult. She wasn't nervous like his mom or snarky like his dad. She was patient and never asked too many questions. But suddenly everything felt at risk because she wanted a full explanation. Pierre reviewed his method to be certain he could trust her.

The key to memory was through sound.

He'd learned about sound by playing the violin.

Mrs. Kimbrough taught him the violin.

Cause and effect.

Yes, his method to recover memory had a direct link to Mrs. Kimbrough.

She was safe.

"Okay. The paper says I heard a falcon call. Later, a rifle shot. I know that because I wrote it at the bottom. And this is the date it happened. That's how I connect things—an event to sounds. Also, I take a picture. These numbers are the coordinates where it happened. We can search the location on the app."

"How did you figure this out? I mean, where'd you get the idea?" she asked.

"It's *my* idea. But it's just logic."

"Ah, *no*. This is much more than logic. It's brilliant."

"Not really. It's science, cause and effect. Anybody could do it," Pierre insisted, shrugging his shoulders.

"I'm not so sure about that. But show me how you find the place."

He took his phone off the nightstand, opened up the lat/long app and entered the location coordinates. Google Earth then displayed where the falcon call and rifle shot had taken place. He handed the phone to Mrs. Kimbrough and she spent some time maneuvering the map.

"Whoa. Wait," she said. "That's the north end of my property. I can tell by this big clearing. See?"

Pierre leaned over and looked at the image. He was disappointed that, at the moment, it meant nothing to him.

"We had some dead oaks ready to fall, so Jim got Luc to help him and they chainsawed the trees," she continued.

She tweezed the screen closer. "Right. Here's what Jim chopped—this stack here. It looks huge in this picture, but it's much smaller now because we've been using it for firewood."

"I think Google Earth updates about once a year, so this picture is probably old," Pierre explained.

"Yeah, that makes sense. We cut the trees down well over a year ago. But according to your paper, someone was using a rifle on my property. And you were there."

"Maybe . . . I don't know. Probably. I don't remember!" he said, feeling trapped.

"Well, you had to be there because you took the picture. That's logical, right?" Mrs. Kimbrough gently suggested.

"I guess," he said with a sigh.

She laughed and rubbed his hair. "Don't worry, you didn't do anything wrong. But it might be worth it for me to go up there and take a look."

"I'm coming with you. You need me for directions." He displayed the phone proudly.

"True enough. I could only guess where that clearing is. Plus, we need you to remember what happened," she said, poking at him. *"Remember?"*

"Lots of times I can't, even using the method," he warned her. "But I might," he added quickly, not wanting to disappoint his teacher.

"That's fine. Anyway, maybe we'll discover who's out with a rifle to-day."

They donned their jackets hanging in the mudroom and headed out the door. She kicked the motorbike into action, and Pierre saddled be-hind her. With his phone as a tracking device, Pierre wrapped his arms around Mrs. Kimbrough's waist and pointed her in the direction of the rifle shot and his memory.

THE MOOSE HAD been roaming on the lands of the small human with red fur and the female human with long white fur, where warm weather had provided enough plant growth to sustain her for quite some time. And the moose sensed safety around these two humans. On this par-ticular day, she'd ventured close to the small human's enclosure, seek-ing salt on the metal containers nearby. She heard noises coming from within. Somehow, the moose could see through an open patch that had been carved into the side of the enclosure. The moose observed the red-furred human lying in a ball. It seemed to be at rest, but then squirmed and quivered and made noises that sounded similar to the distress calls of small animals. After some time, the moose heard a familiar high, grind-ing noise. She smelled the violets, and then saw the female human with long white fur approach on her container. Soon, the red-furred human joined the white-furred human. Together, they headed for the woods on the small metal container. The moose followed.

AMBITION: LOST AND FOUND

SHE RELISHED PIERRE'S ARMS AROUND her as they sped along, and Sandra wondered if this was how motherhood felt. A child glued to her, dependent, yet never a question as to whether he was a burden. In this way, she assumed, a mother and child could never completely lose each other no matter what life brought. That gift of a forever connection was something all her students had given to Sandra. Also, she to them. She saw the evidence on their faces when they mastered a technical difficulty, the disbelief and then joy when realizing that they had *done* it. Or when hearing themselves render a melody with a beautiful sound and then understanding in a split second that *that* was music. Pivotal moments to be remembered forever. Now with the wind in her face, Pierre giggled in her ear and Sandra laughed out loud. He squeezed her waist harder as the motorbike flew a few inches off the ground. At that moment, everything seemed so simple, so clear— to continue teaching and give her students the gift of music. This was Sandra's only ambition.

She'd been quite young when she first heard a parent of a fellow violin student use that word, ambition, and as a criticism against her. No doubt the parent, with typical rivalry, resented Sandra for outperforming their own child. Having no idea what the word meant, she searched the dictionary: "A strong desire to do or to achieve something." That felt unfair and the sting lingered for a long time, because this was not Sandra's nature at all, especially with regard to music. Ambition had nothing to do with how or why she progressed as she did on the violin.

In truth, Sandra was not in control of her gifts. A precocious child, she could mimic entire melodies before talking. A few years after she began to walk, her parents placed the smallest violin available into her hands. She took to it as if it were a superhuman limb, and the speed and depth with which she devoured any music placed on the music stand proved remarkable. Sandra overheard discussions about her unusual talent often, and also whispers that she had something called "great potential." As any young girl might, Sandra wanted very much to please her parents, and especially the violin teachers who nurtured her along the way. But it didn't feel like a hardship or even an obligation. Sandra's progress came with no apparent struggle or stress. Indeed, almost effortlessly.

It was during her years in music conservatory in San Francisco that the word ambition was again aimed in her direction, this time with added nuance—cynicism. And clearly, judgment. As if the fact that she'd blossomed into one of the top violinists in a highly competitive field could not be accomplished *without* a strong dose of ambition. Once again, this saddened her. Sandra was only aware that, though technical facility did come easily to her, interpretation of music was the great leveler. The prospect that she would spend her life trying to understand the essence of music's meaning, and that this pursuit was not some accomplishment to be checked off a list, had always rendered Sandra humble. Yet, she wasn't naïve. Like most musicians, she knew this drive to do well, along with talent and hard work, completed a golden triangle. And to ultimately achieve stature in the music profession, ambition often proved the gang-plank toward success.

Jim and Sandra married the summer after they graduated from conservatory and began to build a decent living as freelancers in San Francisco and the surrounding smaller cities. A few years in, the San Francisco Symphony posted openings for two violins and three cellos, an unusually large turnover. Jim was hopeful, his optimism based on nothing tangible other than his sunny nature, a trait Sandra found particularly attractive and one of the reasons she found him to be a desirable partner. No matter the challenge or the outcome, Jim reasoned his way in and then out, and always with a smile. Sandra, who'd never been a cockeyed optimist, relied on Jim as a ballast point to her own tendencies toward periodic gloom.

With this particular audition though, Jim saw their chances as *exceptional* because of what he claimed were meaningful connections. They knew the conductor from a summer music festival they'd attended while students, a vague association at best. (Sandra doubted the man would remember them, as she and Jim had sat virtually hidden at the back of their respective sections.) Two friends had landed jobs at SFS the previous year. (She easily discovered that neither would be serving on the audition committee and even if they were, she knew they'd surely remain objective in their assessments.) Finally, they already lived in San Francisco, which for Jim was the proverbial nail (proximity being a patently absurd indicator of hometown advantage). But what made all this reasoning thoroughly inconsequential was that major orchestra auditions were held blind, behind a screen. (*No one would even see them,* she thought to herself.) Jim's laundry list of legs up had no bearing whatsoever on their chances. Still, faced with a serious hit-or-miss venture and no better odds than a hundred to one, they both prepared like never before. Practicing hours every day, drilling each other in mock auditions, inviting friends to critique them, taking lessons from elite colleagues. And over weeks of preparation,

Jim reminded Sandra often that with multiple seats open, chances were they'd both land jobs.

The week of auditions arrived. Jim was eliminated in the first-round preliminaries. And it was awkward. He made a reasonable stab at hiding his disappointment and keeping clear, because Sandra was understandably preoccupied with maintaining her game as she continued to advance through multiple rounds. But she heard the tremble in his voice when, the night before her final audition, he insisted that he had in fact totally *aced* his preliminary and was shocked that he'd not passed through. Sandra loved this part of Jim, too—the guileless look on his face when he trotted out unrealistic views about his abilities. Jim was not a top-notch cellist, nor did he breathe music as if it were the oxygen that kept him alive—pretty much a prerequisite for winning a job in a top-tier orchestra. That, and nerves of titanium, which eluded him as well. Sandra had often witnessed him struggle to keep his bow from skittering out of control during high-pressure chamber music performances. Mostly, Jim was blind to the difference between them. While Sandra had the goods in spades, Jim didn't have goods of any suit. The fact was, Jim had bombed and Sandra held both their futures, literally, clamped between her chin and shoulder.

Sandra knew the precise moment she blew her final audition; she flubbed two difficult measures of her concerto—the fingered octaves were badly out of tune. Without even bothering to finish the phrase, Sandra strode off the stage, packed up her violin, and wordlessly walked past the other candidates waiting to play. They peppered questions at her back, because no one walked out like this unless they were crazy. As she pushed out the stage-entrance door, she saw Jim standing across the street. She smiled before he could, then shook her head. He stared at her in disbelief. Then, gathering her in his arms, Jim pulled her close and stroked her hair. He murmured words of comfort into her ear and encouraged her to cry it out, right then and there. With dry eyes, Sandra rubbed her face into his neck and felt her heart beating faster than his while she mentally relived the audition. Maybe she *was* just a little bit crazy.

During the thirty-minute final round, Sandra had experienced an almost epic mastery over her violin. As if it were that fifth limb she'd manipulated with a child's unselfconscious ease. How rare it was that she, or anyone for that matter, could achieve this alchemy of maturity and technical fireworks. At the same time, as she performed for the unseen jury, Sandra sensed an ache in her chest. Not pain or discomfort, but more a kind of nostalgia, like this moment was already in her past. Sadness broke through, as well. But she was playing a particularly melancholy section so in the moment of performing, all these sensations made sense. Then toward the end of her concerto she saw those octaves loom and strangely, her hearing began to diminish. The actual volume of her violin, though very near her left ear, became a whisper.

NO. The word—and she heard it as a warning—rankled her for half a second, but she continued to play with control and beauty. Then the word quickly ricocheted back: *NO, NO, NO, NO.* NO. And Sandra understood what she was meant to do. She played the octaves wrong, off by a mile. *Intentionally.* Small inaccuracies were acceptable during a concert performance, but in the context of an audition where the committee looked for any reason at all to eliminate, the mistake couldn't be forgiven. She knew this very well. Which led to a rare moment of brutal realization. So swift, so stark. Sandra had never, ever wanted an orchestra job. This had always been Jim's ambition for them both. So, having made her mistake, she abruptly stopped playing mid-phrase and immediately felt relief, almost joy. And when she walked past the aghast proctor, another prescient thought came: if she won a position, the weight of their disparate accomplishments—and talents—would become too much for Jim, and this would ultimately doom their marriage.

"What the hell happened in there?" Jim asked after she disengaged from his embrace.

"I completely collapsed," she lied.

"That's hard to believe. You're like a rock."

"To be honest, I never played so shitty."

It was exactly what he needed. Sandra watched him recalculate and then smile broadly, which allowed her to wedge whatever guilt she felt to the back of her mind.

Fleet Week was on in San Francisco. They decided to distance themselves from Sandra's morning flop and wander down to Fisherman's Wharf to watch the spectacle of sailboats dotting the bay. Sitting at the end of the dock, they dangled their legs over the edge. The harbor smelled of diesel fuel mingled with fish. Sandra flinched from the odor and shivered from the strong wind off the water. She scooted closer to Jim and tucked herself next to his warmth. He took her hand and twisted the simple wedding band around her ring finger.

"So, what's plan B?" he asked, clasping her fingers firmly into his.

That Jim could turn the page so easily gave her further encouragement. Sandra was sure they'd get on the other side of this in no time. She rubbed his thigh, her hand settling close to his crotch.

"Continue freelancing," Sandra declared with an upbeat tone. "And keep working on the kid, for sure," she added, turning to give him an impish smile.

Half a dozen rowdy sailors had circled them, crowding their intimate moment, and Jim didn't respond immediately. Once the commotion died down, he stood, pulling Sandra to her feet.

"We can't do that," Jim said.

"What? Not freelance? We're making the rent. And we just got health insurance," she reasoned. "It's going well, right?"

"That's not what I mean."

"Well, what then?"

"I mean the kid."

Sandra cocked her head in a question.

"It's not possible," he repeated.

"Jesus, Jim. I'm off the pill for months now. We agreed."

She reached for him, but he backed away.

"I had a vasectomy. Before we met."

Sandra almost laughed, and searched his face for the joke. But she didn't recognize Jim's expression: his mouth pursed and eyes flat. His Adam's apple pumped once, the swallow his only signal of vulnerability. He blinked and looked away.

Sandra's memory went into overdrive, mostly about the continuous sex they'd had, in service to, so she thought, getting pregnant. At least three nights a week. Many mornings, before either was fully awake. Sex to music because Jim preferred it. Sex to silence, when Sandra insisted on hearing their particular noise of passion. Rug burns when he took her on the floor. Aching muscles from positions she'd endured without so much as a peep. Regular cystitis her gynecologist warned was becoming a concern. Sex talk she couldn't imagine coming from her own mouth (let alone her subconscious). The times she'd sensed that Jim was going through the motions. And now, no wonder.

They fought on and off over the next several days as she tried to convince Jim to reverse the procedure. But his only defense was, unequivocally, that he didn't believe *she* actually wanted kids, either. And Sandra had to look at that, because Jim was one of the most perceptive people she'd ever known; he could dissect someone else's interior life almost on the spot. Plus, there were so many things about their relationship that *did* suit Sandra. He left her alone. Didn't hover. He cooked close to gourmet and was reasonably tidy around the house. He could fix stuff. They both read widely and continuously, a shared passion that was important to

Sandra. And then there was the sex, which had always been pretty great. In the end, Jim provided so much juice to Sandra's life it took her only a week to forgive him. Ironically, through this pivotal event in their young marriage, Sandra discovered the truth about her own ambition: it was immense and knew no bounds. Six months after she lied to Jim about her audition, she guilt-tripped him off the back of his vasectomy into buying the land, sight unseen, in Maine.

Sandra zipped through Oslo woods, maneuvering her motorbike this way and that, dodging trees, bushes, and most of the pits in the ground. Every half minute or so, Pierre checked his phone to track their location and scream fresh directions into Sandra's ear: "Turn right here. Go up that hill. Slow down!" Though she had a general idea where the clearing was, Sandra was keen to follow Pierre's instructions exactly. Giving a child decision-making power was a useful tactic she'd learned through teaching, and most of her students progressed more quickly when asked to set their own goals. Not surprisingly, as soon as Pierre saw that *he* was in control of his own improvement, he tore through his lessons and asked for more demanding tasks each week. With that power shift in place, he'd opened up to Sandra, broaching topics other than music, at times quite esoteric. Pierre was in the process of reading the entire *Encyclopedia Britannica*, and Sandra learned something from him at every lesson. That's when she'd realized how truly curious Pierre was, which from her perspective was a sure predictor of fine musicianship.

Pierre tapped her head, a signal to stop. Sandra switched off the ignition and they dismounted. She got out a thermos of water from the saddlebag, which she always kept handy, and took a swig. Pierre wandered around for a while, turning in circles, looking at the sky, examining horizons.

"Anything?" she asked.

"Nope." Pierre sighed with resignation.

"We just got here. Take your time," she encouraged him.

"Does anybody even know we're up here?" he asked, turning to face her.

"No." She paused for a few seconds. "Does that bother you?"

"Not really. Kinda cool, actually." Then a worried look crossed his face. "It's just that I can't remember if I told my mom."

"She was asleep, so we didn't. But I'm sure she's okay."

"Yeah, I guess so."

"But you remember why we're here, right?" Sandra asked.

"The shots . . . and look! I recognize the border posts!" he yelled, jumping up and down while pointing to the bright-red land markers.

Sandra had to laugh because within the first week of moving to Oslo, Claude had clarified the division of their properties by staking these red wooden posts every hundred yards. Jim saw the move as hostile, and she had to agree it *was* a pretty weird thing to do. And red? They looked like warning beacons in a sea of green: back the hell off. But she'd pleaded with Jim not to raise a fuss, as they were new to the area and unsure of town customs. More importantly, back then the Roys proved to be chilly neighbors, almost distrustful, and she didn't want to test the waters about something that didn't really impact their daily lives. Except Jim's dignity. Then, the ice cracked during a particularly tough winter when Claude's furnace broke down in below-zero temperatures. Because Celine was very pregnant with Pierre, Sandra invited them to stay over until repairs could be made. To her relief, a provisional détente began.

"Nobody does borders like your dad," she said, chuckling.

"Is that a joke, Mrs. Kimbrough?"

"Yes, Pierre, that's a joke. But they *are* a lovely color. Now, keep looking. I won't bother you anymore."

Sandra perched on the motorbike, and Pierre continued to explore. First, he examined the posts as if they were totems with his family history embedded under the red paint. He then scuffed about through low ground cover, searching for clues she couldn't imagine. He consulted the image on his phone again and again, rechecking the horizons in every direction. And just as Sandra was about to suggest they return home, Pierre raced down the hill toward the clearing on Sandra's land. She walked to the edge of the slope and easily located the stacked firewood, which she was relieved to see was sufficient for another winter. Before long, Pierre honed in on one area and began to kick dirt out of the way. Then he knelt to pick something up.

"Come here!" he called to her, waving his clamped hand.

Sandra loped down the hill and stopped just short of Pierre, who squatted beside a swath of dark rust saturating the ground. She inhaled a quick breath and covered her mouth, both involuntary reactions of shock. Pierre turned and smiled. She searched his eyes, expecting him to understand, but his face remained an expression of naïve discovery. He handed over several patches of fur that looked to have been ripped from an animal's body. She fingered them, trying to summon up a reasonable theory. Then the irony struck; it was Pierre himself who, earlier that afternoon, had provided a partial explanation. His memory paper and the rifle shot. She threw the fur to the side and abruptly grabbed his hand.

"It's nothing," she said. "Probably some animal fight. Come on. We should get back."

As they climbed, Sandra spied a parallel path of flattened grasses leading up the hill. Speckled blood had turned green to brown. Pierre saw it as well and pointed. But she pulled him along, even picking up the pace, trying to protect him from such ugly destruction. This was what raising a child must be like, she thought. Harrowing. Every day requiring a million decisions with so much left unspoken because it was more convenient or too awful, like this bloodbath. And now, Sandra herself was complicit. She'd hustled Pierre past where a dying or dead animal had been dragged, all the while acting as if nothing was wrong. Regardless of the fact that Pierre had no memory of this, how strange and sad that he played along.

When they breached the crest, panting from the climb, a man was standing beside her motorbike, his back to them.

"Luc?" Pierre asked, squinting into the setting sun.

"Yeah, Pierre, it's me," Luc said, turning around. "Mrs. Kimbrough," he added, touching his head as a greeting. He brushed a lock of wavy black hair off his brow, which then sprang right back.

"What are you doing up here?" Sandra asked with suspicion. The man stood stock still, his legs like giant cylinders of bread, his arms puffy, even under his jacket. She'd always sensed that Luc could lift a house if the need arose.

"Some chores for Claude . . . he asked me to clear his land."

An explanation of pure foolishness. She gave Luc a dubious look, then noticed he held a rifle behind his back.

"Were you firing that rifle this afternoon?" she asked.

Luc looked to one side and scuffed the ground with his boot.

"What in hell?!" Sandra yelled, throwing her hands up in disbelief.

"I saw a bunch of rabbits and thought I'd get one or two shots off. I didn't hit anything . . ." He tapered off, as if missing his target forgave the behavior.

"It was more like half a dozen at least, and you scared the crap out of me. And God *knows* who else."

"You want me to clear your land, too?" he offered.

"I don't need my land *cleared*, Luc," she said with a sarcasm she doubted he would appreciate. What his specific deficits were, Sandra had never been told. His gram, who loved him with religious devotion, had summed it up—Luc was faithful to a fault. Edna could trust him to step on an ant or run into a fire. Celine christened him as harmless, a non-entity. Jim pled the fifth. For Claude, Luc was a henchman, and he held his job at the March due to Claude's influence. Which was why, Sandra assumed, he was in the woods performing useless chores. Claude had Luc wrapped tight as a mummy.

A thrashing sound behind a nearby grove of trees interrupted them. Luc dropped his rifle and they both ran toward the disturbance to find Pierre crouched close to the ground next to the carcass of a fair-sized animal. His body trembled, and he sobbed deeply in that noiseless way that made Sandra pray for him to take a breath. Luc got behind Pierre and engulfed him in his arms.

"Whoa, Pierre. Steady," he said into the boy's ear.

"Get away from him!" Sandra demanded, trying to pull Luc away.

"I know what to do," Luc said with unexpected authority, and continued to rock Pierre and whisper to him. To Sandra's surprise, his efforts seemed to work. The boy soon relaxed and heaved a final spasm before sitting with his back against a tree. He even gave them both a smile.

Now the scene spread out before her. Sandra quickly deduced that the animal had been killed in her clearing, then dragged up the hill, and finally deposited here with debris thrown around as camouflage. At first glance it looked to be a small deer. Then she saw its rounded snout poking through and fur too dark for a deer. Sandra caught Luc's eyes. He palmed sweat from his forehead and looked away.

"Pierre, honey? Come away from the animal. It's not safe," she said, kneeling down.

"It can't hurt us. It's dead," Pierre protested.

"No, I mean it could be diseased," she explained weakly. "Go back to my motorbike with Luc. Okay? I want to see what's happened."

Luc reached for Pierre's hand, pulled him up, and together they walked away.

The area looked like a battlefield with no winners. She grabbed a few sticks off the ground and brushed away the debris. Now the horror of the animal's death was too evident. The head pointed in one direction, the body in opposition, the legs bent as if still in mid-flight. A catastrophic gun blast to its neck had almost decapitated the thing. No doubt this was the moose's calf she'd searched for while sitting in the truck waiting for Jim. All she could think of now was how truly lucky it was that Pierre had memory lapses. And with more luck he'd forget this entire episode, as well. Then she wouldn't have to explain anything. Sandra, disgusted with herself for having such a thought, threw the branches to the side and walked away from the ruin.

"Where's your truck?" she asked Luc. "You've got tools, right? A shovel?"

"Down that way," he said, pointing toward a road Claude had cleared years ago.

"Pierre, we're going to let Luc take care of the animal. He's going to bury it. He'll be very good to it. Right, Luc?"

"Yeah, I'll give it a nice burial, Pierre."

Before they mounted the motorbike, Pierre took out his phone.

"I want to remember," he said without enthusiasm.

Sandra grabbed it from him and shoved it in her jacket pocket.

"Not this time, sweetie," she said quietly.

She kicked the motorbike to life. They headed south, leaving Luc to bury the moose calf. Trees flew by and the beauty of her land seemed sullied by everything she now understood—Pierre had been there when the calf got killed. She both hated and feared the thought. For the rest of the ride home, Sandra was only aware of Pierre's cheek pressed against her back, her own heart pumping hard in her chest.

THE MOOSE HAD returned to her dead calf every day. She had been waiting for him to rise. Now, the male human with black fur leaned over her calf and kicked his body. He dragged him some distance by the hind legs and heaved him into the back of a large metal container. This sound, her dead calf landing with a heavy thud, disturbed all surrounding nature. Birds ceased chirping. Insects went quiet. Wind died to nothing. The sun above traveled behind a cloud. The entire area diminished in its vitality. The moose watched the metal container travel down the path, her calf's legs waving in the air. She feared for his fate. Would he rise? Would he ever enter the animal world beyond?

HALLELUJAH

CLAUDE CUT THE ENGINE AND COASTED to a stop. He sat inside the truck for several minutes and dragged on a cigarette. When he finally climbed out, he slammed the truck door as hard as possible. Only a murder of crows, dispersing from nearby power lines, reacted to his arrival. Not exactly the species Claude was hoping for. His house appeared as deserted of life as a beach after a shark attack. He leaned against the side of the cab and smelled his fingers. Reeking of smoke, they trembled. His nerves. At the one hospital visit Claude deigned to attend, Pierre's doctor had ambushed him in the men's room to accuse him of causing his family undue *stress*.

Locate your patience.

Ease up on your son.

Try to be an engaged father and supportive husband . . .

These were the suggestions of young Dr. Whatshisname, who'd apparently taken up social work as a side gig to Head of Neurology. At first, Claude indignantly pointed out that *they* were the ones who'd changed, not him. Then, well, they both had their dicks out, so what real choice did he have other than to promise he would try? But the only adjustment to his behavior he'd managed was this door-slam routine—a preemptive warning of sorts. Claude figured whatever the hell was going on in there, his family could damn well sort themselves out and greet him properly. Because what about *his* stress?

Claude lit up again and imagined them actively ignoring him. Pierre was most likely completing his tenth book in as many days. And Celine, all tucked up and sassy in her new bed with her new shoes at the far end of the house (where he entered by invitation only), was surely out like Lottie's eye. If that's the way they coped, goody for them. For his part, he was back to forty a day. Claude tamped down the stub on the sole of his boot and tucked it into his back pocket; his renewed habit was still a secret. Yes, they were in there. He could feel it.

He walked up the stone path and let himself into the mudroom, jammed with at least twenty pairs of rubber clogs, dozens of useless high-end gardening tools, and every kitchen gadget (never opened) known to womankind. Paper grocery bags were stacked floor to ceiling—their re-use, other than as a fire starter, questionable. In fact, he doubted any of this crap would see sunshine before the end of civilization. Claude shimmied through the spoils of a mere fraction of Celine's more recent catalogue acquisitions and entered the kitchen, which appeared much cleaner than when he'd left for work that morning. Claude saw this as a sign that the circus act Celine had performed the previous evening actually meant something.

He'd returned home the previous night at a reasonable hour for a change, and they'd scarfed frozen dinners of mystery meat in about eight minutes flat. As soon as Pierre excused himself to read *Beowulf,* or some such book on animals, Celine dropped to her knees and clasped her hands under her chin. She lifted her face to the heavens and vowed to the lord above that she was done with the pills. Done, done, done. *Done.* Claude's bullshit needle spiked to eleven. She'd promised to ditch the *pilules* on multiple occasions, just one example being a tragic episode involving ice-cream cones in the truck with Pierre. But now, as he recalled Celine's submissive posture and the fact that she *had* prepared a meal last night for the first time in as good as forever, Claude weighed the pros and cons.

On the one hand, there'd been something in her face he'd not seen for quite some time: a determined set to her mouth coupled with a bright-ness in her eyes. Which reminded him of when they'd first met. When she was still a mystery. When he was desperate to understand her nature, which he imagined would ease the ache in his body because he badly wanted to be with her. And the very *fact* of this strange and wonderful ache confirmed for Claude that he'd found a treasure of a woman.

On the other hand, it looked like a botched voodoo ritual gone high Catholic or, more aptly put, a skillet of shit on high heat. Because as long as he'd known Celine, she'd never prayed. Nowhere *near* God-fearing. Yet there she was, genuflecting as if to Jesus himself.

On the third hand, earlier in the day while working his shift at the March, Claude found *himself* praying that he'd return home to that same face. That her willpower was real and so was her promise. Which was probably why he'd stopped at the Robinet, Oslo's dingiest watering hole, to swallow a few shots and chain-smoke half a pack before coming home. To talk himself out of that hope.

Now he looked around the kitchen and shook himself free of any doubt because, *hallelujah*. The dishes *had* been washed and dried, the floor mopped, and mail was stacked on the kitchen counter waiting for his inspection. The napkin holder had been stuffed to capacity, and bot-tles of vitamins (which none of them ever took) lined the windowsill. Even the chairs had been tucked under the table with precise spacing. Celine just might have made it through the first day of the rest of her life after all.

Pleased with this upgrade to his home life, Claude shuffled through some bills and tossed about twenty catalogues into the trash bin. He opened the refrigerator, removed a half-eaten lasagna, and dumped the contents on top of the catalogues—the tomato sauce meant as a deterrent, should Celine spy something irresistible. His stomach growled. He grabbed a cookie from the mason jar and snuck a few swallows of milk directly from the carton. By now, five whole minutes had passed. With his family an obvious no-show, Claude considered his options. He could have a shower, because he stank (but who actually cared?), or hunker down in "his" bedroom to binge on the Hunting Channel.

Then, a lone rubber band on the kitchen table grabbed Claude's attention. The kind wrapped in wrinkled cloth, obviously for a woman with long hair. And this one had silver strands strangling the bright-pink color. Were these *her* paw prints all over his kitchen? Come to think of it, he *smelled* her. Violets. Saint Kimbrough. *Merde*. After a soul-crushing shift featuring an argument with Luc about that damned dead moose calf, and then drinking and smoking himself into a dither at the Robinet, it seemed a man couldn't even return to the comfort of his filthy kitchen. Claude's hope promptly took a kamikaze.

He stuck his head into Pierre's bedroom. MIA. Not exactly a surprise. Still, it stung. More deflating, the boy's room mirrored why he felt like the weird uncle who visited every third year. Books smeared across the bed. Music volumes stacked on his desk. That godforsaken violin propped in a corner. He perched at the edge of Pierre's bed, dragged his hands through his hair, and allowed himself a *rare* moment of self-pity. The details of his son's life, and the fact that none of it rang a single cowbell in all of Maine, brought up a terrible sense of alienation. He felt useless, and a fraud. His nerves. The March. His family. The *stress*. And then, there was Luc Sibley and that dead moose calf.

Luc had been Claude's pet project and ongoing disaster since Edna asked that he secure him a job at the March. The mill wasn't union, but a long history of nepotism made it as good as. A man had to just about kill somebody to get fired from the March. And it was easy enough to squeeze Luc in, since Claude was a shift foreman and wielded power. Before too long, Edna wanted more—would he *mentor* her grandson? Her term. And why not? Initially, the man's slowness appealed to Claude. Luc was malleable and settled into his bottom-level rank at the March nicely. That Claude used Luc from time to time for his own purposes, well, he saw it as hazard pay. And at this point well deserved, because Claude discovered soon enough that Luc operated in ways that didn't yield nearly enough to justify mentoring him. But the most annoying thing about Luc Sibley was, in order to shift the man's ass into overdrive, commands had to be stated over and over. And over.

"There's a dead moose calf up north on my land. I need you to pick it up and bring it down to the shed," Claude had ordered a week earlier.

"Uh-huh," Luc said, eyes veering to his left.

"Look at me. Get yourself up to the northern end of my property."

One nod.

"Find that moose calf."

Slow nod.

"Bring it down, clean it up, butcher it."

No nod.

"Luc. Pay attention. Get that animal down here before it goes gamey."

Multiple rapid nods.

Simple head movements, Claude knew, didn't necessarily translate into action. So.

"Okay, here we go. Three time's the charm. You're gonna use my truck and drive up north on my road. Right? You'll find the dead moose calf behind a clump of trees with leaves and stuff thrown over it. Easy. Then you're gonna bring it directly to the shed at the far side of the March. No detours. Lay it out on the table and carve the thing up. Just like I taught you. Okay? Then wrap it up and throw the meat in the freezer. Got all that? Do it today. Like, now."

"You got it, Claude," Luc assured him.

"Go on, then. Get it done. And remember, mum's the word."

"Huh?"

"You're on the QT."

"Um . . . what? I mean . . ."

"It's a secret! Don't tell anybody."

"Oh. Right."

Claude had left Luc alone for the entire week, figuring he couldn't possibly mess it up, what with three distinct sets of instructions. Big mistake. Because earlier that morning, Claude discovered the freezer in the shed was empty. He stormed through the March, which took about fifteen minutes, and then finally found Luc in the bathroom taking a pee. The man was midstream, so Claude waited till he zipped up and then muscled him into a stall to rectify a now potentially risky situation.

"What the hell, Luc? It's been a week. Is that moose calf still in the woods rotting its way into oblivion?"

"Yeah, probably."

"What does it take for you to follow simple orders?!" Claude yelled.

"Sorry." Luc flicked the seat down and sat.

Claude loomed over him and pointed to Luc's crotch. "Sorry helps about as much as your limp dick."

"I meant to do it, but Gram said—"

"When're you gonna act like a grown man? That's what I've been trying to teach you."

"I know, but see, Gram had me on lots of errands this week. I guess I forgot . . . ," Luc stammered, now standing and shifting from foot to foot like he needed to pee again.

"Your gram put me in charge of you. That means *I'm* supposed to be your priority."

Luc slumped back down on the toilet seat and palmed his eyes.

"Look at me," Claude said.

Luc opened one eye through two fingers.

"I got you this job, for Christ's sake. Plus, I taught you the ropes, saved your ass a bunch of times. Am I right?"

"I guess."

"Sure I'm right. But you gotta do as I say. Now get up there today. Bury the thing. And bring me a token—an ear, a tail, a hoof—*anything* so's I know you've done it. And if I don't find a body part on my desk tomorrow, you'll be on shit duty for a month." He flushed the toilet with a stomp of his boot to reinforce Luc's potential job demotion, and walked out.

Claude lay across Pierre's bed in a fetal position, his knees clamped to his chest, praying that Luc had buried that dead moose calf today. Dust from his work clothes had migrated to the bedspread, and he knew this would disturb his boy. Pierre didn't like anyone messing with his room, which was organized in a way Claude found frightening. He got up and brushed the debris onto the floor, then scuffed it under the bed. He straightened out the covers and fluffed the pillow. Satisfied that his presence would go undetected, Claude stomped through the new addition of the house. He stopped short of Celine's bedroom, took a few preparatory breaths, and braced for what he might find. He eased the door open. There she was, asleep. Naked and posed like a pole dancer, her arms tangled above her head and legs bent at improbable angles. Her face was aimed toward Claude's, almost like she was expecting him. He leaned in, inspecting the entirety of the woman he wanted to be with till the end of days.

She didn't need to tweeze her eyebrows, her arches still as shapely as the crescent moons he'd likened them to when they'd first dated. Back then, he believed such imagery was his only chance to get her into bed. After about a week of struggling for fresh material, the quality of which had fallen off directly after the moon idea, Celine told him not to bother—she liked him just fine. Still, she'd held off sex till the honeymoon and Claude had never desired another woman since.

Snoring had become a new habit for Celine. Now, her wet snuffle sounded feminine, almost sexy. Claude grabbed a tissue and wiped her nose of snot. She squirmed and licked her Kewpie lips. And he wondered why she bothered with the dozen-or-so lipsticks stacked three-deep in the medicine cabinet. In fact, makeup in general served no earthly purpose on Celine. The way she appeared right now, even in this stoned sleep, was about as good as any sight God had ever created.

She threw out a phlegmy cough and stretched mightily, craning her neck. Though beginning to mottle, that neck was always his starting point when they made love. Kissing the skin just under her chin made Celine laugh like a hyena, a sound he hadn't heard for weeks. His eyes then traveled to her nipples, which had darkened from breastfeeding Pierre twelve years earlier and remained so. Claude had been jealous of this particular attention to their infant son, an absurd notion, he knew, and was still ashamed to admit. Now, he'd give anything to return to that time. When their house had just the original four rooms, and Claude had installed a rocking chair in each so she could nurse Pierre anywhere. And now, he couldn't help but stare at her pubic area, and for a second felt like a sick voyeur because his dick grew chubby. But *mon Dieu*, Celine was still as beautiful as a chiseled Venus-de-whoever. Still, his dear wife.

Since Pierre's accident and the subsequent weeks of Celine's decline, Claude wouldn't let himself call her an addict, because she still managed some very good days. But a lack of hygiene seemed her latest slip. She'd discontinued daily showers and had taken to wearing the same clothes every day, maybe even the same underwear for all he knew. Even so, it wasn't so bad, because Claude still wanted her. He'd inhale her underarms, her oily hair, and her sweet funk, which always both surprised and reassured him. He'd ignore the dirt under her chipped fingernails and tolerate the scratch of her unshaven legs. He'd even forgive that she'd let her bikini-wax grow in, something he'd gradually gotten used to and now preferred. Mostly, he'd be happy if she'd just wake up, right now, and show him the same bright and hopeful expression from the previous night, when she'd bowed to Jesus and promised to Claude that she was *done* with the *pilules*.

Celine stretched, moving like molasses. With her eyes still shut she repositioned herself to face the wall. Claude floated a blanket over her. He settled next to the bed in the sole surviving rocking chair. Exhausted and lulled by the staggered breathing of his wife, Claude fell asleep.

Dusk had filtered through the room when Claude woke. Celine, now sitting on her bed wrapped in her robe, was watching him.

"Get out," she hissed.

"I was just checking your pulse."

"Sometimes I wish I were dead." Celine whispered the words into her lap.

"Where's Pierre?"

"He's not here?" Her lips trembled and she began to tear up.

"You've nothing to do all day except raise our son."

Celine began to climb off the bed but Claude stopped her with the toe of his boot. She slumped back against the wall and he felt like a brute. Then he remembered the violets.

"Where is my boy?" Claude asked evenly.

Celine primly adjusted her robe. "I fell asleep after I picked him up from school. Probably with Sandra?"

"Wonderful," he said, shaking his head at the ceiling.

"She cares about him."

"She's snoopy. Sneaky."

They stared at each other and he wondered how to proceed with the least amount of blood. Claude thought, *Uncle,* and kissed at her through the air. She swatted it back.

"When does he visit that brain quack again?" Claude asked.

"He's called a neurologist. In a day or two, I think."

"My God. This so-called recovery has been going on for *weeks,*" Claude whined.

"He needs to rest and heal. You can't control this one."

"Let me lie with you?" It popped out as if to no one in particular. Claude fully expected to meet a pout, but she granted him a quarter smile and he crawled in next to her. They spooned. He was grateful. And for about thirty seconds, sex seemed possible. Then, she slipped her feet into a pair of Michael Kors and scuffed down the hall.

Claude followed Celine to the kitchen and sat at the table while she foraged around for food. He rubbed his fingers over the table's rough surface. Maybe he'd sand it down and then shellac it, something Celine had been bugging him to do for over a year. Maybe he'd have her pick the stain color. Maybe Pierre would help, or simply hand him the different grades of sandpaper as needed. The idea of home improvements family style buoyed his mood, until he realized he might as well make plans to win the Maine Megabucks lottery.

"Aren't you gonna at least call Saint Kimbrough? See if he's with her?" He'd be damned if *he* phoned that household.

She had her head stuck in the refrigerator and pulled out a platter of something. That she didn't notice the lasagna was gone was some relief. The microwave dinged and Celine divided the meal onto two plates. The food stared at him, light brown in color. Was this beef or chicken? Claude, ravenous, stuffed in a mouthful. It singed the roof of his mouth, and his eyes teared from the pain. He threw his fork on top of the food.

It wiggled.

"Okay, so don't call. But who cleaned this place up?" he asked.

"Pierre is clearly with Sandra," she said with a sigh.

"Well, it's getting dark. He shouldn't be out this late. It's a school night."

"School's finished."

"Since when?" Claude stared at her.

"Crawl back under your rock. Please."

His fingers twitched, not so much from the conversation, which was circling the drain fast, but because his craving for a smoke was driving him mental. He rubbed his face vigorously, scratched his mustache and shook out his hands—anything to confuse the jones. Celine gave him a sympathetic smile, reached into the cabinet beneath the sink, and pulled out a pack of Camels from Claude's hidden stash. She tossed the pack at him. He caught it with two fingers.

"Your little 'secret,'" Celine said, making air quotes.

"Busted," Claude said as he plucked one from the pack and lit up.

He stretched out his legs, sucking deeply, and observed her from across the table as she picked at her food. Her robe had sloughed open and now he noticed that the gold heart on a chain he'd given her the night before they married was missing. She'd never taken it off as far as he knew, even to shower. He searched her face and wondered whether this was the correct moment to be offended or even curious. Then she gathered the lapels of her robe together with her fists and leveled her eyes at him.

"I had nothing to do with it," he said quietly, trying to head her off at the pass.

"Don't give me that!" She shot up from her chair and rocked on the balls of her feet. Her body looked taut and unpredictable, and Claude instinctively raised his arms like a defensive boxer.

"What do you want from me? I wasn't *there* when it happened," he repeated emphatically, then paused several beats. "I can't do this again, Celine."

She sat back down and took a breath with gargantuan effort, then released the air slowly like a leaking bicycle tire. She made a pretense of wiping the corners of her mouth of food; she'd barely taken a bite. While she went through this ritual meant to calm herself, Claude braced.

"All your time at the March, no one so much as breathes without you knowing."

"You think too much of me."

Celine slammed her palm on the table. "Pierre has 'fallen' at the March. You have no idea how it happened. That's just not possible."

"He'll get better. You said yourself, he just needs time," Claude said.

"And I'm going batshit crazy." Celine scooped up his cigarette pack and let them trickle to the floor.

Claude listened to the scrape of her heels diminish until she stepped into the bathroom and slammed the door. The medicine cabinet didn't screech as he expected, and the sink faucet remained silent. Shortly, the toilet flushed. Claude hoped she'd recede to the other end of the house.

"You tell me what happened right now," she demanded, sitting back down.

"I told you. I wasn't there."

"I'm going to watch you hurt for this," she said.

He shrugged weakly and felt a thick shudder power through his body. The urge to run out of the house, the town, the state, the country, was frightening, because she'd never threatened him this way before. Since Pierre's accident, the more Claude had tried to convince her he wasn't responsible for his injury, the more she'd dug in. And her persistence surprised him, because their marriage was one of the good ones. Especially in the way they tacitly agreed to an ebb and flow of marital accommodation. And no matter how improbably stretched those agreements were at times, he mostly did his part and Celine always did hers.

Claude sank to his knees and scooted around the table. He pried her legs open and pressed his torso close to her body. The contact lacked any pulse of sex. In fact, right then he felt as ignorant of the world as a newborn. She allowed his face to settled at her belly and he breathed in the smell of her robe, a cagey combination of laundry soap and week-old sweat. Celine then pulled his face up toward hers and touched her nose to his. She clawed her fingers through the tangles in his overgrown hair and let out that hyena laugh. Claude groaned.

"You need a cut."

"I'll do it tomorrow," he promised.

And just like that his world pivoted on how Celine still loved him, and how he desperately needed her to believe him. Because the story he'd told, again and again, was the truth. He *hadn't* been there. Claude could repeat those words to Celine any time of the day or night, and not be a liar. But, of course, Claude knew exactly what had happened and that his illegal trapping business was at the center of it all. And now he heard the Saint's motorbike approaching fast, almost like a thin army battalion, and knew that his son was aboard. It slowed, and Claude was relieved when the noise grew again as she sped away. Pierre opened the door and smiled at them.

"Where you been, honey?" Celine asked.

"Out for a ride."

"What'd you do?" she pressed.

"Some stuff. Really fun stuff."

Whatever he'd done and wherever he'd been, the boy didn't remember a damned thing. Claude was certain of it. *Just a while longer*, he thought. *Then I'll stop the business.*

He squeezed Celine closer and gestured for Pierre. The boy raced toward them and they had a group hug. Celine started to sing the song

"Hallelujah." Pierre joined. Singing had been a bedtime ritual for them when he was younger, the Leonard Cohen a favorite. Pierre's soprano range hovered over Celine's quiet mezzo, which made the song sound innocent. It was a word Celine would approve of and a word Claude would normally fight about. But innocent, he was not. Claude was just grateful that right now, Pierre seemed to remember that his parents still loved each other.

NOBODY'S HOME

EDNA SIBLEY STOOD ON HER WRAPAROUND porch and stretched out over the railing while simultaneously peering down the winding driveway. Not that she could see very far. Her house stood purposely secluded, sited among a variety of large firs and wildly overgrown hydrangea trees. Despite seeing nothing, she was usually able to hear anyone approach from a one-mile radius, whether by car at the front, or via boat on the lake side. Years ago, she'd done the math and clocked it. Since most in Oslo knew every pothole and bend on the lake road approaching her home, speed was typically thirty miles per hour. With this assumption in place, Edna calculated a generous two-minute lead time. More than ample to scoop up a soiled glass or two, straighten the growing stack of *New Yorker* magazines she'd recently neglected, crimp loose wisps of hair into her bun, and smudge on some lipstick. Even swap out her garden mucksters for pumps, if she sensed it might be desirable.

Luc occasionally performed the odd errand for Claude, and Edna assumed this was the reason he was now late for dinner. Though more frequent of late, she could easily forgive these delays, because Claude had become an important male role model for her grandson—in fact the only one he'd ever known. Edna, being a woman and so much older, questioned her ability to guide Luc appropriately, and so in this respect she had much to be grateful for in Claude Roy, who had agreed to provide that authoritative presence. Even so, she couldn't help but fret about Luc's current tardiness. Rather than sit for lunch at the March cafeteria, she knew that on most days Luc raided the candy machines that littered the hallways, substituting countless chocolate bars throughout the day for a proper mid-shift meal. Candy was a terrible habit, of course, but her real concern was that when Luc did arrive late for dinner, he'd be ravenous. Hunger often triggered his tremors.

Waiting well over an hour now, and with Luc still nowhere within sight or even earshot, Edna worried the pearls at her neck. To distract herself, she stepped into the house to check on the table setting. Standing at one end of the dining room, Edna admired how the embroidered Irish linen runner, a treasured gift from her late husband, was sufficiently long to span the fourteen-foot cherrywood table and still drape the appropriate eight-inch excess at either end. Two salad servings, consisting of chopped iceberg lettuce, carrot scrapings, and razor-sliced radishes for zest, sat to the side of Wedgwood dinner plates. Edna liked this blue-and-white pattern for everyday meals. A chest-on-chest cabinet housed her eighty-piece set of eighteenth-century Sèvres china, though Edna hadn't brought that out since her daughter, Samantha, was alive.

Sammy, as she was called, had been a terribly picky eater, refusing most meats and even the standard vegetables: peas, carrots, and the like. When Edna discovered that her six-year-old found delight in the elaborate red dragon painted at the center of every Sèvres piece, she used the fragile tableware as an enticement. Sammy quickly devoured her meal so that the creature could emerge from beneath the food. Then she'd invent intricate stories about the dragon, who soon became her imaginary best friend. Edna sacrificed too many plates to breakage, but Sammy ate.

Luc, thankfully, hadn't inherited his mother's persnickety eating issues. But aside from that, there wasn't a reason in the world to use that china now. The smart dinner parties she and Edgar hosted were long-ago memories, and even the thought of such an event now tired Edna. She palmed a streak of dust from the table surface and wondered if the local thrift store would take such an enormous grouping of dinnerware, albeit incomplete. No, they'd most likely break it up for the convenience of multiple sales. She'd wait to place the entire collection with the right person, someone who really understood the aesthetic and historic significance.

But details of any meal still required Edna's close attention, a rite she hewed to, what with being raised in a Boston Brahmin family. Hidden Valley Ranch was Luc's favorite salad dressing. She preferred generic Thousand Island, which she then enhanced with minced pickles. Both had been puddled into Japanese dipping bowls with tiny spoons canted on the edge, now resting near their respective salads. Edna wouldn't allow the ketchup bottle anywhere near the dining table until Luc had finished his salad and was poised to tackle the meat portion of the meal. If left to his whims he'd use that condiment on virtually all food—steak, pork, fowl, fish, eggs, toast. Even certain donuts. The mere existence of plastic bottles (much less one sitting on the table), not only went against her patrician upbringing, but Edgar, too, would have had a fit. The least she could do to honor his memory was return the ketchup to the kitchen immediately after Luc drowned whatever food was on his plate.

Throughout dinner preparations that afternoon, Edna had taken breaks to lounge on her private dock by the lake. She finished the final entry of *The Diary of a Nobody*, a book that had begun at a snail's pace but eventually drew her in. Edna was known in Oslo as a voracious reader, and Celine had asked her to vet "controversial" books for Pierre. His interests had recently expanded well beyond his years, and Celine admitted she was out of her depth as to what to allow. Privately, Edna didn't believe in filtering what a child showed interest in. These constructs and restrictions were more indicative of adult limitations, though in Celine's case, she was very bright—just not a reader. Edna had given a solid thumbs-up on all the Salinger titles without rereading them, her own silent protest. In any event, she'd spent the last few days previewing *Nobody* for Pierre, who'd expressed skepticism about the very idea of a living person being a *nobody*. Also, Pierre posited, if someone were truly a nobody, he doubted their so-called diary would get published in the first place. Edna admired the first notion, which skirted concepts of existentialism, and she couldn't disagree with his doubt regarding the logic of publication. And now that *Nobody,* in fact, proved harmless, Edna found herself eager for Pierre to read the book so they could discuss such satire. In so many ways, Pierre Roy was a delight to have around. He pushed her envelopes much the way Sammy had.

Nobody sat on one of the dining chairs. She tossed it into a nearby satchel of Pierre's to-be-read collection when she noticed, with no small amount of distress, deep wrinkles crisscrossing her cotton skirt. The ups and downs and back and forth of the afternoon's activities had distorted the beauty of the floral chintz fabric. Worse, splatters of gravy from the meat loaf warming in the oven had sullied the white background color. How careless that she'd selected this outfit, which she saw now was much too dressy for an ordinary day at home. Edna vigorously smoothed out the creases with her palms, making a mental note to donate all her floral clothing, which comprised a good fifty percent of her wardrobe, to Goodwill. The next day wouldn't be too soon. These days, flowers depressed her.

She walked the length of the dining room, noting that the toile wallpaper had discolored at the ceiling and was due to be changed. And she had to laugh at herself, because she'd been observing the same condition every week for at least six months. Refreshing any decoration before it grew too worn was, she knew, a habit of the wealthy. Yet Edna didn't feel especially privileged, nor was she immune to hardship. Pastoral wallpaper would never bring back Edgar, and she wondered why the grief she still felt after all these years hadn't subsided to the bearable state so-called experts assured her it would. All the china in France hadn't prevented her sixteen-year-old daughter from dying an hour after Luc's birth. And now, even a mile of Irish linen couldn't ensure that her grandson would be safe in the world after she herself died.

As much as people tried to hide their snickering, Edna knew Luc was seen by town folks as a simpleton who was very, very lucky to have a rich grandma. And with her wealth, he did have it better than almost everyone in Oslo. But Luc's challenges, not particularly obvious, were significant and required a great deal of forethought. Because of this, Edna spent most of her days advocating from a state of hypervigilance, the dining-room table being just one example.

She'd positioned the two place settings at a corner. Necessary, because Luc was not comfortable sitting opposite anyone. General eye contact seemed to be almost unbearable, and in fact at some point during most conversations he'd turn his entire head. And then there were tremors, which the doctors assured her were not due to epilepsy. But they'd never been able to diagnose the origin, whether neurological or some psychological imprint. These were just two of several behavioral conditions Edna had described in detail when Luc was young and diagnoses were still being proffered. One by one, all were proven incorrect. In the end she was left with, "We just don't know about Luc." What was she supposed to do with that unhelpful string of words?

Edna slumped into a dining chair, nestled her head into her arms on the table, and closed her eyes. This early evening fatigue had become routine. Most birds were silent late in the day, but she heard a single loon calling every ten seconds or so from across the lake. Edna found herself waiting for each hoot, and in doing so, dropped into a shallow sleep. She dreamt lightly about her daughter standing on the porch waiting for Luc, just as she had less than an hour before. Then, oddly, Luc's approaching truck broke through with a growing hum, and she roused herself.

Now Edna was behind schedule. She hurried into the kitchen to turn up the oven so the meat loaf could be served at the correct temperature. Then she worried that the roast had dried out, so she grabbed a baster from a drawer and sucked up the juices. A few splatters landed on her blouse. She swatted at the stains with a dishrag, which embedded the grease even more. She'd just destroyed a perfectly good silk top, her entire outfit now nothing less than shabby. To mask her carelessness, she donned Edgar's old chef apron, still hanging on a hook in the pantry. Edgar had loomed a good foot and a half taller, so the apron reached Edna's ankles. *My God.* With her mucksters sticking out below she not only felt a fool, but now looked the part too. After positioning the ketchup on the kitchen counter closest to the dining room, Edna ran out the front door. Luc had already backed his truck into the space next to her car.

"Wait, Gram. She's almost done," Luc said, tapping his fingers on the steering wheel.

Patsy Cline. Edna never imagined country music within a fifty-mile radius of her house, but courtesy of Claude Roy, Luc was now fond of her. While she waited for Patsy to finish falling to pieces, Edna glanced at the back of the truck. Two legs with cloven hoofs pointed in the air in a vee formation, like a victory salute.

"Luc!" She reached in and switched off the radio.

"Yeah, Gram?" he answered, staring out the opposite window.

"Get out of this truck right now."

Luc eased himself out of the cab and they walked to the rear of the truck.

"Explain this," she demanded.

"It's a moose. A baby."

"I can *see that*." She paused and forced herself to look more closely at the animal. "My God, Luc. It's been torn to bits! Tell me you didn't do this."

"I found it," he said, examining his boots.

"Where."

"Up north."

"North? What do you mean?"

"On Claude's land."

She prompted him with her hands, like directing traffic. "Come on . . . more . . . *explain*."

"I was cleaning. For Claude."

"Oh Lord. That's utter nonsense and you know it."

She sighed heavily. There was no point in pursuing the extended Q&A needed to extract information while standing beside a dead animal. Anyway, her more pressing worry was Luc's hunger.

"Come inside. Dinner's waiting. And leave your boots outside. They're *filthy*."

"Right, Gram."

They ate mostly in silence, which was their habit. Luc chewed his meat loaf with a steady rhythm. Having no appetite, not unusual of late, Edna picked at her salad and thought more about that poor animal. She felt angry, but not terribly. Confused, certainly. Mostly, Edna didn't like surprises—and this one, so grisly. And there'd been other perplexing episodes. Like Luc accompanying Claude to unspecified places where he "warmed the truck seat." For what purpose, instinct told her not to grill Luc or even ask Claude. Yes, murkiness lurked, but also surprising breakthroughs. Luc described, and in exhaustive detail, the ongoing renovations to Claude's house, the most bewildering structure she'd ever laid eyes on. In fact, a true horror. Edna couldn't understand the first thing about what Claude was trying to accomplish. How this layout would in any way be suitable for his family, or why Celine would even agree to it, Edna was at a loss. Regardless, after a work session at the Roys', Luc would return home chattering on about every nail, every hammer, every paint color. All the progress they made. How Claude left him alone, trusted him to do the work. And that even when he messed up, which Luc admitted was a lot, Claude let him fix it. She'd never seen her grandson so deeply interested in something, other than the TV programs he was addicted to and had committed to memory. Edna glanced at Luc, now engrossed in his mashed potatoes. He stopped mid-forkful, looked up at her, and smiled. There it was: pure sweetness. He was her best boy who, when she so wanted to give him everything, asked for absolutely nothing. Edna had to trust Claude. She saw no other way.

Their plates sat, his wiped clean, hers full. As night came on and the houses across the lake began to flicker, Edna waited for Luc to explain about the baby moose.

"I messed up," he finally confessed.

"I'll say. My God, I can practically smell the thing from here."

"Not like that."

"How, then?"

"With Claude."

"Keep going."

"Claude told me about the baby moose last week. But I forgot. And then this morning he reminded me. He got mad."

"But for pity's sake, why'd you bring it here?"

"I was hungry. And I was driving. So . . ."

"In that case, you did just the right thing. You understand?"

"I know, Gram."

Luc wiped his hands on a cloth napkin and was about to drop it onto his plate. Then he quickly refolded it, setting it to the side. He dropped his head. She watched him work through his discomfort from failing Claude and disappointing her. But she was greatly relieved that at least he showed some level of self-awareness about hunger being connected to his tremors, and got off the road.

"Okay, honey. In the morning we'll go to the March together and talk to Claude. We'll settle it—the three of us."

Luc nodded and appeared satisfied with her assurance. He picked up their plates to do the dishes, a chore he enjoyed.

"Gram, you didn't finish."

"I know. I had a big lunch," she lied.

"Should I dump it?"

"Might as well."

"Okay, Gram."

"I'm going up to bed. You'll remember to lock the doors?"

"Sure, Gram."

Edna left her mucksters by the bottom step and climbed the stairs, tripping twice on Edgar's apron. In her bedroom she pulled the apron off, folded it into a square, and stuffed it under Edgar's shirts in the bottom drawer of his bureau. She let her skirt drop to the floor and toe-kicked it to the side of the room. The pearls at her neck felt hot to the touch. She undid the clasp and placed them into her everyday jewelry box. After she unbuttoned the stained blouse and draped it over the back of the chair by her vanity, she decided she'd throw out all her silks along with the florals. What had she been thinking all these years? She lived in Maine, not Beacon Hill.

She unclipped her bra. Two foam inserts bounced to the carpet and landed somewhere out of sight. She stood in front of the mirror in just her underpants and forced herself to look. The breast surgeon had worked to get the incisions lined up in a reasonable horizontal, but small flaps of excess skin had since marred his effort. The plastic surgeon had pressed her to have a reconstruction, but there was no point. The last person to touch them in any way that meant something was Edgar, the night before he died. They'd made love after their daughter, then only a few months old, fell asleep. Per her feeding schedule, Sammy's cries woke Edna at three in the morning. As she nursed her downstairs in the kitchen so as to not disturb Edgar, whom she knew had a busy day ahead, Edna heard a thump on the floor above. Her daughter became enraged if taken from the breast before she was sated, so Edna waited a full fifteen minutes for Sammy to finish. She found Edgar lying at the threshold between the bedroom and the hallway, dead of a massive stroke. He'd tried to get to her. Edna's milk mysteriously dried up within a week of Edgar's death. Sammy struggled to get used to formula, and then later with food until the day she died. How could Edna explain to the plastic surgeon that her breasts had always reminded her of death? In truth, she was glad to be rid of them.

No one knew of her cancer. Oslo gossip had a life of its own and Edna couldn't chance even Sandra, whom she felt close to. She'd shielded the entire episode by having the double mastectomy performed in Boston, with the excuse of needing ten days to attend to complex estate issues and various charity board meetings. No, her cancer, which she'd recently learned had metastasized, was gossip she'd not gift to the town of Oslo.

Edna's sense of smell and taste had diminished somewhat due to the new chemo pill she was taking. But the odor of the dead animal wafted faintly into the room, or so she imagined. Though it was a warm evening, she closed the windows. She floated a lacey nightgown over her head and down her body. She pulled the covers back and lay on "her side" of the bed, farthest from the door and potential intruders. Edgar had been the best husband, always protective. She stretched one arm out to his side of the bed and stroked the empty pillow.

"Oh, my darling. Tell me what to do."

THE CIRCUS COMETH

GRADUAL DOWNSIZING AT THE MARCH
had all but eliminated proper offices for shift foremen like Claude. But
he'd needed privacy for his business, so he hijacked a room at the end of a
remote hallway and fashioned it to suit his purposes. His desk sat hidden
behind several tall lockers, blocking the door but allowing enough space
to squeeze by. Should anyone surprise him, he'd have time enough to
throw all damning evidence in a drawer and present an innocent smile.
And Claude was basic—no computer. He entered the numbers by hand
into a bound ledger, and always with a 4B pencil, the softest lead available.
Pink Pearl-type erasers ensured the cleanest changes. That he didn't like
sloppy or crossed-out payroll columns was just one thing Claude had
learned about himself; on paper at least, Claude was a neat freak. Even
more surprising, the high he felt running the trapping business was close
to a perfect buzz—that headspace where you'd had a few shots and might
go ahead and get snorting drunk, but then you thought better of it and
ended up feeling fucking virtuous in the morning. Weighing pros and
cons, reasoning things out, making calculated decisions, none of that

could be explored as a company man at the March, whose routines hadn't changed much in years. Claude thrived on the tension hidden inside of risk.

All he had been going for at first was a bit of mad money. Maybe surprise Celine with jewelry normally out of his reach. With that bling long since satisfied, they were now neck-deep in footwear. And who knew Celine had been binging *Project Runway* reruns and had a thing for Tim Gunn (or was it Zac Posen?) and any shoe with a minimum four-inch heel? For Pierre it was one thing only: a college education, which had somehow become a foregone conclusion. According to Celine, the very idea of "her" son following in Claude's footsteps at the March was *ludicrous*, a word Claude thought overwrought but conceded to because he couldn't handle another synonym battle. Though, even if the boy got accepted to some super-expensive hoity-toity school, which everyone in Oslo expected he would, Claude now had enough cash, literally under his mattress, to get Pierre through four years of college. Maybe. Probably not. Actually, Claude had no idea what college cost.

But nothing was easy. Annoyances popped up, mostly about keeping his small crew in line. Every few months they'd make noises about wanting more of the profits. And who could blame them—greed was almost as huge an urge as sex. But they also wanted to discuss things, be part of the process, have *decision-making* power. It took brains to both toss them bones and fend them off at the same time. And damned if he hadn't developed actual sympathy for the owners of the March, who for years had successfully squashed unionizing. Claude now understood what they'd always known: if you gave people a voice, they developed opinions really fast. And that, almost without exception, mucked stuff up.

Claude was now at his desk and had just finished preparing for the weekly meeting. He ran his finger down several columns and checked them one more time with the calculator. The sums appeared to be correct.

And impressive, because after paying his four-man crew double wages, plus a flat fee to the lobster guy from the coast who trucked the meat downstate (his industry had also hit the shitter), Claude's personal profit was better than usual. He snapped the book closed, slid it to the back of a locker, took out a roll of bills, and clipped the bolt lock shut.

They filed into the tight space and circled around him, sipping coffee dregs before the next shift change. As Claude doled out money to each man, he recapped the week's spoils.

"We brought in some nice stuff," Claude said. "About a dozen rabbits and a good-sized doe. Four grey fox. And two badgers."

"*Badgers*?" one of the men said, laughing.

"I know, but the meat can be used for somebody's dog. Who wants 'em?" Claude asked.

"I'll take it," another man said. "My hounds go for that stuff."

"Good. That's about it for now. The traps all reset for this week?"

"We did it yesterday."

"Okay. Moving forward, I wanna give you guys a heads-up. I'm thinking about winding down the operation. Maybe stretch it out through summer and then disband early fall."

The men, while saying nothing, nodded noncommittally.

"What, no comments for a change?" Claude asked.

"Not really," the man with the hounds said after a few moments. "We figured it's been coming."

"Huh," Claude grunted, not knowing exactly what he meant. "Well, that was easy," he said, laughing.

"It's been a good ride," the hound man continued.

"Good enough?" Claude asked.

"More than we ever expected."

"So, no one has a strong objection? Because whatever we do, we have to be in lockstep. I don't want anybody going rogue."

The men shook their heads, shrugged agreeably, and left just as the shift bell rang.

Oddly, he hadn't planned on announcing that day. But it seemed his crew was ahead of him, and it left Claude feeling relieved. He'd always warned them that if the business shut down, it'd have to be like it never existed. And now with their unanimous agreement, he felt grateful that he wouldn't have to babysit the one guy who was greedy and disgruntled and would surely cause problems down the line. He propped his feet on the desk edge, satisfied with his leading skills, or whatever that jargon was, and watched the shift transfer from the window. Then he jumped up out of his seat. *What in hell?* Claude was certainly surprised to see Edna with Luc, who'd pulled up just then. But he could never have predicted that moose calf in the back of the truck, its legs akimbo for all creation to see. Claude stared in disbelief. In the name of Lucifer, what was Luc doing showing up with that dead moose calf?

And what a sideshow, like the Keystone Cops. Luc rushed over to help Edna from the cab. She shooed him away with typical pride and jumped down, then stumbled a few feet before righting herself and dusting off. Despite her age, Claude considered Edna still beautiful, a faded cover girl. But the really great thing about Edna was that after she voiced outrage for about thirty seconds on any topic, she was pretty reasonable for a rich lady. And under normal circumstances, if Claude just waited her out, he could convince her of anything. But my God, how was he going to fix *this*?

Claude sat back down and watched the Sibley circus finish up their routine. Edna continued to flap about, laying down her instructions non-stop, while Luc nodded whenever she took a breath. Rinse and repeat. The woman was practically a midget; she had to tilt her head all the way back just to meet Luc's face, which was turned to the side per usual. The difference in their height had always struck Claude as odd. He wondered where Luc got his six-foot-plus frame, because he recalled the daughter as being a shrimp just like her mother. The husband, whom Claude never met and whom Edna still talked about as if he were the pope about to walk through the front door and shove a wafer down someone's throat, must have been the culprit. Now, though still spouting some blather as if it made any difference at all, Edna looked to be running out of energy. When he was certain she'd completely blown through her head of steam, Claude walked outside.

"What's all this?" he asked, strolling up.

"Oh, good, Claude. Luc brought this thing home last night and I could barely sleep from the stench. *Look* at it. Dreadful," she said, poking at her bun.

"I told you to *bury* this thing," Claude said to Luc.

Luc bowed his head and clasped his hands behind his back like he was preparing to be handcuffed. He began to shift from foot to foot and if Claude hadn't known better, he'd call it a jig.

"What I want to know is how it died," Edna broke in before Luc could respond. "I mean, this is *ghastly*. Take a look, Claude. I'm a novice . . ." She trailed off.

Claude took a deep breath and held it as he walked to the back of the truck to examine the dead animal. He was in luck. The scavenging and decay were so extensive Claude couldn't locate the gunshot wound he'd inflicted. Relieved, he let out his breath.

"No big deal, Edna. It's the wasting disease—the deer tick that makes them go batty. I found the thing dead about a week ago and asked Luc to take care of it. Guess he forgot. So here we are. But it does stink something mighty. Let's get ahead of the breeze."

He took Edna by the arm and guided her away from the truck. Luc stayed back, apparently not bothered by the smell.

"That means you, too. Get over here!" Claude yelled.

"*Claude.* So harsh."

"Seriously, Edna, how's he supposed to learn?"

She fumbled with her pearls and looked at her wristwatch. "I'm sorry. I'm not myself at all. I dropped a dozen eggs on the kitchen floor this morning. And I've got to get to Shaw's before all the supposed fresh produce is snapped up. We're out of ketchup. Claude, you need a haircut. And shouldn't Luc start his shift?"

"Take it *easy*, Edna," he said, running his fingers through his hair. "Luc! Get on your shift!" he barked.

Edna jumped up to plant a kiss on Luc's cheek, missing by a mile. Luc gave them both an oversized smile and a stiff wave goodbye. Truly, the man was a mystery, Claude thought as Luc shuffled away.

Edna grabbed Claude's upper arm, her red fingernails digging into his bicep. "Claude. If that calf got the tick, where is the cow, the mother? Poor *creatures*."

"Don't try to understand these dumb animals. It's a waste of time. They go here and there, willy-nilly, and then one ups and dies. And now look what's happened. You've lost a night's sleep over it. This is no good, Edna."

"You're right. I can't seem to relax. My mind's a jumble. And I'm so worried about him, Claude. You have no idea."

"Luc? He's gonna be fine. You'll see. C'mon. Let's get you to the store."

Claude looked around the parking area and spied one of his crew sitting in his car reading the newspaper. He ushered Edna into the passenger seat. She smoothed her dress and primly crossed her legs, canting them to the side. Claude noticed she wore only one earring, and her knee protruded from an enormous hole in her stocking. She had on mismatched high heels. He'd never seen Edna this disheveled or more befuddled. "I'll talk to Luc," he assured her, patting her hand.

"You will?"

"I just said I would."

"But, will you . . . *really?*"

The degree of sadness in her face startled Claude. He gently closed the car door and walked over to the driver side. "Jerry, take Edna on her errands. Shop with her. Then take her home and help her unload the groceries."

"Sure, boss. Shaw's?"

Claude nodded, then leaned in and lowered his voice. "And make sure she's all settled in. Maybe suggest she take a nap."

Edna fussed with her hair, then completely unraveled her bun and rested her head on the side window as Jerry drove away. Luc was inside waiting for Claude, and he walked him back to his office.

"What in Christ's name happened up there?" Claude asked, sitting on the desk.

"Mrs. Kimbrough. She messed me up."

"Whoa. What does the Saint have to do with this? Wait. Go back to yesterday. Nice and slow."

"I found the baby. Just where you said."

"Good. Then what?"

"Well, see, I took my rifle with me. I tried for some rabbits . . . that's not so bad, is it?"

Claude sighed, because he'd probably do the same thing. "Fine. And?"

"Mrs. Kimbrough heard the shots. She came up on her motorbike. With Pierre."

"My *son?*"

"Oh no . . . ," Luc whimpered, covering his mouth.

"Jesus. *What?*"

"He cried."

"Why!?"

"He saw the baby. All torn up."

Claude jumped off the desk and pushed Luc into a wall, pinning him by the shoulders. He didn't want to hurt him, just scare him a little.

"So, Edna knows about that moose calf. The Saint knows about that moose calf. And now my *son*? This is a huge problem, Luc. People talk. And I don't like any talk about animals, alive or dead. Why is that?"

Luc began to quiver—his shaking. Claude released him and sat back down.

"Take a stab," Claude prodded.

"The business?"

"Bingo. And what kind of business do I run?"

"Trapping?"

"Uh-huh. And what's special about that?"

"It's not legal?"

"Right. But why in the name of Satan didn't you bury that thing yesterday like I ordered?"

"I wanted to show you," Luc whispered, aiming the words toward the floor.

"Show me what?"

"My idea?"

"God help me. More?"

"I remembered what you said once."

"This better be good."

"You told me to take chances."

"Lordy."

Luc finally lifted his head and, oddly, leveled his eyes directly at Claude. "I figured if I brought the baby back to the shed, we could use the skin. Like we do with the other animals. I wanted to show you. I can think of things, too. I'm not so dumb."

Luc's mouth pouted, on the verge, holding back an emotion Claude did not want any part of. He could smell the man's distress and it wasn't pleasant.

"Listen to me. I'm not your parent, but I'm trying to help. You know that, right?"

"Yeah."

"I don't need your ideas. At least not yet. Maybe soon. But when I give an order, you're to do it. So, here's a new order: get that moose calf over to the dump right now."

"Not bury it—?"

"*Stop*. Do exactly as I say. I want you back in less than an hour. I'll cover for you. *Go*."

Claude punched Luc's time card and walked the eleven minutes to the other side of the March to do some wood-chip loading, the very job he'd started on right out of high school. As he eased back into the rhythm of muscle memory, Claude considered the possibility that he'd not fully understood Luc's limitations. Further, for some reason, Luc seemed to be suddenly growing a set of balls. And ironically, that very morning before Claude left for work, Celine had called him a person of *staggering* limitations and also questioned the state of his "manhood"—code for testicles. Apparently, his self-professed confidence was about as real as a spider's dick. He couldn't think ahead, and she only had to point to their house— the holy grail of impulsivity—to prove her point. Finally, all he could muster with regard to "her" son's memory loss was to be a bro-friend. In other words, leave all the heavy lifting to her, and more recently, the Saint. Then she sobbed for a while, after which she begged him to run to the store for milk, which he did. He'd left the house in a lousy mood because it seemed that the hallelujah-kumbaya the three of them had achieved the night before had not stuck. And he still needed a haircut.

While thinking that his life had become some kind of perfected shit show, Claude had relaxed his vigilance. Something in the machinery bucked, and he staggered back. He shoved his goggles up and wiped his face of sweat. The din in the March suddenly felt unbearable, and he frantically searched his pockets for earplugs but found none. As if to punish him for giving his last pair to Luc the previous day, the noise now doubled in volume. Claude backed up against a wall and slid down to a sitting position. His head dropped to his knees. The drill in his ears, the wide tremor of his hands, and the way he couldn't catch his breath, well, this was exactly what had happened to him the day of Pierre's accident.

When Claude had first arrived at the hospital, he looked right and left, frantic with the hope that Pierre would run up and grab him by the legs as he usually did. Instead, at the end of a hallway he saw a cluster of doctors and nurses. Hugging the wall was a stretcher with a small body lying beneath a sheet. Pierre's sneakers hung at the end, pigeon-toed like always. When the sneakers began to twitch, a nurse stroked Pierre's arm and the doctors leaned over his face. He then noticed the sneakers jiggle faster, as if a flame had been lit and Pierre was flinching from the heat. That's when he heard his boy moan loudly.

Claude had seen all this as he walked down the corridor with Edna. It seemed an endless trip during which an unimaginable future poured into his mind. If Pierre died now, he wouldn't meet his first girlfriend, whom he'd love with an almost painful urgency. And he'd not marry a woman whom he'd try very hard to make happy but would fail many times. And then, he'd never get to experience that drop-to-his-knees relief when this wife decided to hang on in spite of all the agonies in their marriage. She'd love Pierre no matter what. Claude was certain of this. That is, if his boy lived.

He stopped short of Pierre's sneakers and stared. Edna took his arm. He thought she needed the support, but in fact her grip was surprisingly strong. He closed his eyes. She slid her hand down to his, then squeezed and pushed him a few inches forward. His hands began to shake. His breath went shallow. The siren started between his ears. When he opened his eyes, the space now seemed very large and too bright. He noticed a stripe on the white wall, a baby-blue color, and he wondered what that color was meant to make people like him feel. Ordinary people. People who didn't want to be there but were, due to circumstances beyond their control. Or maybe circumstances they themselves had caused. Then Claude saw the blood, thick and congealed, covering every last strand on Pierre's head. His left eye was shut. No color in the natural world came close to his boy's painted eyelid. Claude sank to his knees and Edna went down with him.

"Will he die?" Claude asked no one in particular, surprised that he could even speak.

"No, not at all. We've got him lightly sedated so we can run tests and determine where he's damaged. It looks worse than it is." Someone said this, but Claude didn't know who.

"But his legs," Claude whimpered from a crouched position.

"That's just a sympathetic reaction, Mr. Roy. It's normal when the brain has been jostled."

He got through the next hours in an embarrassing trance, almost speechless, and was grateful that Edna took over. With an almost psychic ability to predict when Pierre needed help, she paged the nurses. When he needed to ask a question, Claude immediately ceded to Edna, because he *had* lost his voice. And just as her authority was evident to everyone in the room, his own weakness appalled him. But Pierre was released that day with a purple eye and a knock to his head. They promised that he'd be just fine.

Claude sat on the floor of the March, waiting for the buzzing to subside and his heart to stop pounding. He clasped his fingers together, willing his hands to settle. He glanced up to see Luc's boots scuffing toward him. Claude now remembered that at the hospital he'd concentrated only on those boots, afraid of what he might do if he looked into Luc's eyes.

While Claude walked the eleven minutes back to his office, he repeated the truest words he knew:

I wasn't there. I wasn't there. I wasn't there. I wasn't there.

WHEN THE LARGE human with black fur appeared with his metal container at the place where crows and buzzards scavenged on dead things, the moose had been waiting. The area smelled of death well past its time, and her calf had already reached that same state days earlier. Now, the large human with black fur pulled her calf out of the metal container. He flung him by the back legs and her calf separated, midair, into two pieces. The head landed in one direction, still visible to the moose. The rest, somewhere beyond. There was nothing more to be done. Even in this dismembered state, her calf would rise. The moose turned away.

ALL THE LOONS

CARS BACKED OUT OF PARKING SPOTS ON
either side of Room 222 at the Loon Motel. Celine flopped onto her back
and glanced at the clock—twenty minutes left till checkout time. Her
feet always cramped after an orgasm, so she flexed her toes while trying
to remember what was on the grocery list she'd forgotten when leaving
the house earlier that morning. Milk. Obviously. Bread. No-brainer.
Not much else came to mind. She'd swing by Shaw's on her way home,
and hopefully walking the aisles would prompt her. As a fallback, ready-
made dinners in the gourmet section would do fine for that evening.
Especially if in the moment of shopping, the thought of cooking dinner
felt as improbable as it did right now. Meat, casseroles, the oven. Plates,
forks, the dishwasher. Paper-towel squares standing in for napkins. All
of it, a drudgery. Anyway, who was she fooling? Celine hadn't prepared
more than a handful of meals in the last month. In fact, all household
tasks she used to perform as a matter of rote, and even enjoyed, she now
shirked. Celine felt a failure as a homemaker, an identity she'd always
taken pride in. And as a wife, she was nothing more than a cruel harpy.

Earlier that morning and before either of them had coffee, Celine had gone after Claude's manhood. She laughed at and then derided the size of his penis, which in truth she quite admired. But oh, how she wanted him to suffer for everything that had gone wrong. Which was not an easy thing to accomplish, because Claude was the least repentant person in the state of Maine. He'd make the hardest cider out of rotten apples and remain cold sober. Plead the fifth. Innocent as a lifer on death row. Introspection was just another word for "are you kidding me?" In other words, Claude was *all* good, *all* day long. But that morning, as she'd shoved him into every dark corner of their marriage, Celine could tell he was at some sort of brink. Still, that didn't stop her from nailing him in the only place he'd hurt. His dick.

The walls at the Loon were no better than two sheets of cardboard glued together. She listened to the couple who'd just arrived next door discuss a puppy that had gone missing. And while they worried about Kelly the Labrador, Celine wondered where in hell her brand-new Dyson vacuum cleaner had gone to. The previous night, intending to take advantage of a rare surge of energy and clean the house, she'd searched every closet. AWOL. So, she rimmed the perimeter of each room collecting any dust bunny bigger than a golf ball. Claude trailed behind, pointing out those she'd missed. Meanwhile, Pierre, after losing a coin toss to Claude, busied himself with five loads of laundry. And Pierre being Pierre, his color sorting was intuitive, his choice of water temperature spot-on. And folding, a wonder of origami precision. Now, rhythmic moaning from next door had supplanted any concern for poor Kelly, and Celine doubted she'd make it to Shaw's. And though she suddenly remembered where the Dyson was (the garage, for some reason), how in the world was she going to convince Claude that his dick was just fine?

Water began to flow in the bathroom with characteristic sputtering, the Loon's pressure notoriously unpredictable at peak morning use. First a trickle, then intermittent pulses, and finally a middling stream. She would have liked to join Jim for a quick rinse, but showering separately (when he mentally eased himself back to Sandra-land) was just one of the many rules he insisted on. Such as, the first and third Tuesday of each month. Two hours. Max. Pay in cash. Only. No phone calls. *Ever*. If either of them couldn't make it, wait fifteen minutes, then leave. And, park in the back. Always.

Jim walked out of the bathroom naked, with a towel draped around his shoulders. He stepped into boxers and drew up the blackouts to let some light in.

"Why aren't you dressed? Time's almost up."

"Let's stay another hour," she suggested. The Loon was that kind of motel—pleased to accommodate those renting by the hour.

"Why? What for?" he asked.

"Why not?"

"A dozen reasons, starting with rules."

"So over*raaaaated*," she said, howling a yawn.

"Do you hear yourself? I mean about the rules."

"You sound like Claude."

"Don't be like this, Celine," he warned, poking his legs into jeans and gathering up his keys and wallet off the nightstand.

"Now you *really* sound like him," she said, turning away and scrunching the covers up to her chin. "Claude's rigid. Don't be like *that*."

"That's a cheap shot."

"I don't care. *Please*."

Begging was becoming a habit of hers and a problem for Jim. A month earlier, she'd asked him to switch their regular Tuesday to a Wednesday because she had to take Pierre to the doctor. With the appointment two weeks out, she felt certain he'd make an exception. But Jim would have none of it. Rules were sacrosanct, and if it meant they skipped a session and as a result didn't see each other for an entire month, so be it. His point being, don't mess with a routine that had worked perfectly for going on a year. But Celine continued to wheedle and accused him of being inflexible, especially in light of "the reason." That did it. He accused *her* of using Pierre to manipulate him, which *was* objectively true. They ended up screaming at each other. Someone pounded on the wall. And for the first time ever, they didn't have sex.

So, this morning, Celine had been bent on making things right. She jumped on Jim the minute he walked into the room. In fact, she practically chewed his clothes off. Ferocious she was, with inventive foreplay. Ears? Why not? Toes? Um, sure, there's a first time for everything. And before intercourse, she pushed him down to give her head. The first orgasm was real. The second? Well, until that morning Celine had never faked anything with Jim.

He sat on the bed and nudged her in the back. She turned toward him and offered a hopeful smile.

"Don't get the wrong idea. I'm leaving in a few minutes," he said, tapping his watch.

"You don't know me," she whispered.

"I believe I do."

"Then why can't you understand that I *need another hour*?"

He scrunched his lips in a grimace and she could tell he was trying to decide, or something worse. Maybe he knew the second orgasm was a sham . . .

Jim reached over her and picked up the phone. "Marge? Give us another half hour."

She giggled, not quite believing that Jim had actually broken one of his own rules. He dug his keys out of his pocket and threw them back onto the nightstand.

"I'm here. What?"

"Everything Claude says about me is true," she said.

"He's a psychopath."

"He's not."

"Then a sociopath."

"But I *am* a terrible mother. I couldn't find the vacuum cleaner—"

"*What?*" Jim said, incredulous.

"We haven't had sex. I'm pathetic."

"That doesn't make you pathetic, it means you're discriminating."

"I'm so cruel to him. A monster. You have no idea. I owe him at least a fuck."

"Marriage doesn't work like that, Celine."

"Yes, it does. Exactly that way," she said, wiping fresh tears away.

"Oh wow," he said after a long sigh. "What am I going to do with you?"

She flopped against his chest and bawled like a newborn having an asthma attack. Jim held her face and kissed her between sobs, trying to get her to stop. Finally, crying became hiccups and Celine, eyeing the clock, forced herself to calm down. Only seven minutes left.

"Pierre loves Sandra . . . I'm jealous," she confessed, snuffing back snot.

"Everybody's jealous of Sandra. *I'm* jealous of Sandra."

"She's the only functioning adult he knows."

"So . . . this is about Pierre?" he asked, thumbing moisture from her upper lip.

She shrugged with an exaggerated motion, holding up her shoulders. "Maybe. Yeah, probably."

Celine caught herself in the mirror opposite the bed, looking like the queen of hags. Stringy hair, mascara smudges, sunken cheeks. Ashamed that her breasts, which had lost buoyancy due to recent weight loss, sagged badly.

"How can you even *stand* me?" she asked, pointing to herself.

"Oh, you're so repulsive. *And* difficult," Jim said, laughing.

"It's not funny."

"Yes, it is."

He picked up the phone and ordered another hour from Marge, and for the first time in the year they'd been secret best friends with benefits, Celine told Jim she loved him.

"Love makes liars out of people," he said quietly.

"It's not a lie."

"I know it."

He'd never say it back, she knew that well enough. But within this room, filled with all the risks they rarely spoke about, Celine hoped that extra time at the Loon was Jim's smoke signal for love. He gathered her up, squeezing her so tight she almost lost her breath. And she imagined he was physically willing her to make it through the next minute, hour, day, week.

"You good for a while?" he whispered into her ear.

"Yeah," she grunted.

"I didn't bring any. Can you last till next time?"

"If I'm careful."

"Go easy."

"I'm trying. *Really.*"

Jim's eyes welled up and he hid his face with his hands.

"It's not your fault, Jim. You gave me the first one. I took all the rest."

"I could kill myself for doing this to you," he said, his voice cracking.

They fell back onto the bed, where Celine's crying was overpowered by Jim's sobs.

THE DAY OF Pierre's accident, Celine had been scrambling to find someone to pick him up from an after-school event. The other moms on her call list either weren't available or didn't answer. Claude was useless, because reception west of the Hump and at the March was almost nonexistent unless he happened to be standing exactly in one of three hot spots. For a few minutes Celine considered abandoning her plans and picking up her son. Then, in a final stab at getting coverage, she called Edna.

"Luc's out back trying to get our generator cleared out from the windstorm. So many *branches*! Did you and Claude suffer?"

Edna always began a phone call with updates on either the weather or what Luc was doing that very moment, or both—a formality that, though endearingly Edna, annoyed Celine on this particular day because she was in a hurry.

"No, we're fine. But I heard some folks in Peru had terrible damage."

"Always *something* up here in Maine—"

"Listen, Edna, sorry to rush you, but I have a favor to ask. Pierre will be waiting for me at school in about thirty minutes, and I'm tied up. Is there any chance Luc could scoot over and pick him up?"

"I'm *sure* he can, but hang on a minute."

Celine heard the phone clunk on the counter and then some distant shouting with Edna-like emphasis on every sixth word or so.

"Celine? It's fine. I'll have him leave in five minutes *just* to be on the safe side."

"You're a doll. Thanks."

She'd returned home no more than two hours later, expecting Pierre to greet her at the door. He was old enough to stay by himself for short periods, especially with Sandra and Jim just up the road. But the house was empty, and she immediately felt uneasy. Celine waited only ten seconds before calling Edna, who didn't answer the phone. This set her to a panic because Edna, a disciple of schedules, was always, *always* home at that time of day.

Celine raced to the school on the off chance that Pierre was still there, though she knew the trip was pure folly. Indeed, the parking lot was deserted, and the front doors had been chained. She idled for a few minutes, trying to conjure up even one plausible reason that Pierre was just fine. She knew he wasn't. There was no option but to head toward the center of Oslo and specifically, the police station. She jammed the gas, running a few red lights along the way. When the road leading to the hospital appeared on her left, on impulse, she careened toward the emergency entrance. She parked right next to Luc's truck, almost hitting a light pole in the process. Edna's car was nearby, straddling two spaces at a sloppy angle.

Then came a sequence of events which, in weeks to come, she'd dream about over and over and in unbearable detail. Slamming the car door and then realizing she'd left her purse on the seat. And thanking God she had the keys right there in her palm. But leaving the purse there anyway, because at that moment she spotted Claude's truck near the hospital entrance. And pushing through the glass doors, stumbling to her knees, ripping her pants leg while simultaneously tasting blood because she'd bit her tongue. Edna and Luc huddling at the end of a corridor. Claude walking toward her much too slowly. His eyes so wide, from a man who was never, ever surprised. And Celine collapsing to all fours, her head hanging like a beaten dog. Because she *knew* her son was dead.

Pierre was released from the hospital that night with a hopeful prognosis—the doctors had assured them he'd be good as new in no time. But the very next morning, Celine realized her son was facing a planet of trouble. Not with his purple eye. Not with his aching body. Not with his lack of appetite, nor even his unquenchable thirst. But all that he'd forgotten. Not only had Pierre lost the entire day of the accident, but large chunks of his general memory seemed to be missing, as well. By early afternoon, after badgering the doctors all morning, who advised nothing more than to wait and see, Celine broke one of Jim's rules for the first time. She called him at home.

"How is he?" Jim asked, interrupting the first ring as if expecting her. The news had spread through Oslo by this time, and she and Claude were fielding dozens of calls from well-wishers.

She sobbed into the phone, unable to speak for a long minute.

"*Tell* me," he said finally.

"He can't remember anything," she managed to blurt out through tears.

"Confusion?"

"*No*. When we came home last night he went right to sleep. No idea about the memory loss until this morning. I think it's very serious, Jim."

"Shit."

"But that's not it. I mean it *is* . . . but . . . I can't get anybody to tell me what happened."

"Not Luc?"

"Only that he had to take care of something at the March and made a detour before bringing Pierre home. He claims he left Pierre alone for a few minutes and when he came back to get him, he was on the floor, unconscious. That's his story."

"It's possible, though—"

"Don't defend him!"

"Calm down, Celine. I'm just trying to work it through with you. Rationally—"

"I don't believe him. Luc is obedient like a dog, especially with Edna and instructions. But more and more he's been *glued* to Claude with this mentoring thing. And now Claude's been skulking around the house like he just beat his own mother to a pulp. He might not have been there, but he knows what happened. I *know* that man."

"Is it possible you're overreacting—"

"*Stop*!" she screamed.

To make the call to Jim, Celine had secreted herself in a storage closet, and she suddenly felt suffocated by the wool winter coats on either side. Though the closet itself was cool, Celine began to sweat and felt close to blacking out. Now she could hear Jim panting over the phone, almost in sync with her own breathing.

"I have to see you. Please. Do this one thing for me," she begged.

"Not at the Loon. Can you get to Portland? Tomorrow?" he asked.

"Of course. *Yes.*"

"There's a Motel 6 just outside of town. I'll reserve a room . . . about two-ish."

Celine arrived at the Motel 6 unwashed and hungry. Jim pulled out a sandwich from the pocket of his cello case and forced her to eat it. He ran the water and helped her into the tub, then washed her hair with Dial soap from the pump. Celine couldn't stop shivering, so he added hot water from time to time. Finally, her body seemed to release the tension she'd been holding from not sleeping for over twenty-four hours. Once in bed and under the covers, she turned onto her belly and wailed into the pillow. Jim dragged a desk chair over and waited her out. When her voice got too hoarse to make much of a sound at all, he reached into his pocket and pulled out a vial.

"Take one when you get home. It'll help."

"What is it?" she croaked.

"Painkiller. For my back. It'll put you to sleep."

He tapped a dozen small white pills into her palm.

NOON APPROACHED AT the Loon and a chambermaid knocked twice.

"We're still in here!" Celine yelled.

A faint "sorry, senorita" came from the other side of the door.

"Look at us. We're both wrecks," Jim said, blowing his nose. "At least Sandra's in Portland today, so we don't have to worry about the extra time."

"Claude never asks where I've been anymore. He's terrified of me. And all guilty about Pierre."

"Well, he should be. I mean about Pierre," Jim said.

"Lighten up on Claude."

"Are you kidding?"

"Jim, I have to get this out. Tell you something."

Being the only one naked, Celine suddenly felt modest. She got up, pulled on her clothes, and sat on the only chair in the room. A Gideon Bible lay on the desktop and she considered picking it up, but somebody else's god couldn't help her now. Jim eyed her with a worry she'd never seen on his face.

"It's not what you think," she assured him.

"What do I think?"

"That I'm having sex with someone else. I mean, other than Claude."

"Good. Because that's exactly what I was thinking."

"It's worse."

"Nothing could be worse than that. Unless you killed somebody. Wait . . . Claude?"

Usually Celine appreciated Jim's dark humor, and he often joked about Claude disappearing one day like Jimmy Hoffa. But she couldn't laugh now; nothing had been funny for a long time.

"It was my fault. I caused the whole thing."

"That thing being . . ."

"Pierre," she said, biting her fingernails.

"You mean his accident?"

"I stopped to get a manicure."

"Huh? You could use another," he said, leaning forward and gently slapping her hand away from her mouth.

"And then I got a pedicure."

"I have *no* idea where this is going—"

"They hadn't dried enough. My toes. So, I figured if somebody was available for a massage, I'd get one while they dried. But that was going to make me late to pick up Pierre, so I called Edna and got Luc to pick him up. All because of my fucking toenails."

"Oh, *come on,* Celine—"

"Wait. It gets worse. Then I talked to the salon owner for another thirty minutes. By the time I left, Pierre was already in the hospital."

Jim stared at her, shaking his head in disbelief.

"It's my only job. To be his mother. To keep him safe. To pick him up from school. To not get pedicures—"

"*Wait.* Are you stoned right now?"

"Not since yesterday. I told you. I'm trying."

"Good. Now I'm sure you'll understand this. A million things could have prevented Pierre's accident that day. A *million* things . . . *including* Luc bringing Pierre directly home. You are not responsible, Celine. Don't make this your problem."

The problem was, once upon a time the pills actually did their job. She slept as if unconscious, then woke and functioned as usual. But as Pierre's condition dragged on and her family disintegrated in front of her eyes, Celine wanted to shut it all out. Even the hope. She began to chip. Now the problem was that Jim's notion of the truth felt empty. His answers to her problems, no matter how rational and well-intentioned, had ceased to mean what she knew they should. Because the only answer that made any sense at all, seemed to be a pill.

A RED-SLASH DAY

MORE AND MORE, PIERRE'S MOM (AND occasionally his dad) had been interrupting his practice sessions, bugging him about unimportant stuff like, had he brushed his teeth? (Yes.) Or, did he want to help shop for food? (No.) And, most irritating, had he gotten any memory back? (No comment.) So, Pierre had recently devised a method to get rid of them. As soon as he heard footsteps approaching from down the hall, he'd close his eyes and play as loud as he could. They'd try and try and try to talk over the sound, even poke him on the shoulder. But if he just kept playing and ignored anything they did or said to make him stop and pay attention, sooner or later they'd back out of the room. He'd then refocus, continue practicing, and soon forget all their pointless questions. That was the best thing about playing the violin: getting lost. The sounds, and music, were Pierre's safe zone.

This morning he was working on an especially tricky passage in the last movement of the Vivaldi concerto. He tried to play it correctly three times in a row, something Mrs. Kimbrough said he should aim for. She said three was a special number—even called it "spiritual"—and that it was also connected to physics and lots of other stuff. Mrs. Kimbrough warned that three was a very hard thing to do. Pierre was skeptical. But he soon discovered that while twice in a row was pretty easy, three *was* almost impossible. He'd just started the fifth round of attempts, when a banging on the mudroom door broke his concentration. Pierre ignored the noise and now decided to pick apart the phrase. Slowing it down, he played one note, then the next and the next, focusing only on his bow arm. Then he brought in the left hand and tried for accuracy of pitch. Finally, he added the correct rhythms. Each thing on its own was really hard. But when all of it *did* come together, oh, how that made him happy.

Now he was ready to try another round of three, but the door pounding hadn't stopped. He took his time. He wiped his violin with a soft rag and placed it on the bed; Pierre meant to come straight back to practicing once he got rid of whoever was at the door. Then, he squared up the small area rug, which had gone off-kilter, and straightened a fresh stack of books from Edna. Just as Pierre walked out of his bedroom to see who was there, the banging stopped. Still, he wanted to make certain they were gone.

"Is your mom home?"

Mrs. Cabot stood next to the Ringleader, who was all dressed up with colored bows in her hair and green toenails poking out of her sandals—obviously trying to bring attention to herself. Pierre suddenly worried that he'd forgotten something. Maybe his mom had scheduled some weird playdate. Pierre grimaced at the thought. He didn't want friends to be organized for him and had told her so many times.

"Yeah. But she's busy," he said.

Mrs. Cabot started up the three steps to the door as if she expected to come inside. They'd never been to his house before. At least that's what Pierre assumed, though he couldn't be absolutely certain. It *was* possible his mom had Mrs. Cabot over as a friend. That is, back when his mom did that sort of thing. But the Ringleader? No way he'd ever allow *her* into his house. Pierre stood directly in the center of the door frame, blocking Mrs. Cabot.

"Oh. Okay. Sure," Mrs. Cabot stuttered, backing down the steps. "It's just that we had a ton of leftovers from last night's dinner and thought you all might enjoy them."

Pierre eyed a large platter the Ringleader held in her arms. She extended the food in his direction. Her fingernails were the same color as her toes, another sign of "look at me" disease. All the mean girls seemed to care about this matchy-match thing. Pierre thought it was ridiculous.

"What is it?" he asked Mrs. Cabot, ignoring the Ringleader.

"We're leaving tomorrow on vacation. The food will go to waste," Mrs. Cabot continued without answering his question, something Pierre hated about adults.

The Ringleader, who'd been staring mostly at her green toes all this time, finally lifted her head and threw him her trickiest, phoniest, most evil smile to date. And Pierre suddenly knew the real reason they'd driven all the way to his house. Delivering their half-eaten food, as if they were *poor,* was just a diversion tactic. The Ringleader wanted an excuse to torture him one more time before they went on their stupid vacation, to rub his nose in the fact that her family had money and was way better off than his family. Yes, that was it.

Mrs. Cabot huffed a few times, still expecting Pierre to move aside to let them in. No way. Finally, she grabbed the platter from her horrible daughter and shoved it into Pierre's arms.

"Thanks. I guess," Pierre said.

He watched them drive off and when they were a safe distance away, Pierre peeked under the foil. He was hungry—maybe the food was halfway decent. Shriveled mushrooms, smelly cheese, and a bunch of other useless food like celery, which had no taste at all so why even bother? He flung the food out the back door for the birds and jammed the platter to the bottom of a garbage pail.

On the way back to his room, Pierre detoured into the new wing to listen at his mom's bedroom door. They were talking about the length of her dress and whether or not she should wear a belt, because his mom had lost weight. Even through a closed door, Pierre could tell his mom's mood just by the tone of her voice. Sloppy talk, like thick soup plopping into a bowl, meant she'd taken a pill. Peppy, like boots crunching on hard snow, meant it might be a good day. Then Pierre heard his mom laugh at something Mrs. Kimbrough said and they both giggled for a long time—a hopeful sign. Relieved, he returned to his room and instead of practicing more, Pierre decided to read Edna's latest approved book, *The Diary of a Nobody,* which was finally getting good.

Shortly, he heard their footsteps approach. A quiet tap on his door, which then swung open. They both displayed smiles—too wide, too many teeth. When adults smiled like this, something was about to happen. Usually annoying, sometimes bad. But his mom looked pretty, so maybe not so terrible. Her eyebrows were filled in with pencil, and pink dotted her cheeks. The dress she wore had flowers all over, the same shade as her eyes. Mrs. Kimbrough was fancy, too. They were obviously going someplace together, though Pierre couldn't begin to guess where.

"We're going to the doctor," his mom said as if reading his mind.

"It's not on the schedule!" Pierre wailed, pointing to the large monthly calendar his mom had nailed to the wall so he could "remember" upcoming appointments. The plan had been that she'd draw color-coded diagonal slashes for activities she thought should mean something to him. Red slashes were for doctor visits, always a bad day. Blue for everything supposedly fun, like the swimming lessons he secretly hated—but couldn't tell his mom because it would just make her sad—because the Ringleader was in his diving group. Green meant violin lessons, the only thing he actually cared about. The square for today's date was empty. No red slash.

His mom stared at the calendar and fussed with her hair, which Pierre noticed had been washed and curled. He loved it when she managed to bathe, even if Mrs. Kimbrough helped like she had that morning.

"I'm sorry, honey. I guess I forgot," his mom said.

"It's okay. But *all day?*"

"Just the morning this time, I promise. They're going to repeat the tests to see if there's been improvement."

He didn't care what the tests showed—they wouldn't change all the things that had gone wrong. His mom was usually sloppy and mostly sad and never cooked. His dad hardly came home, and when he did, just argued with his mom in her bedroom. *Those* were the things that needed fixing, not his brain. Pierre then noticed the next day on the calendar had a green slash. He pointed to it and looked at Mrs. Kimbrough, who nodded.

"You ready?" she asked.

"Uh-huh. And I have a surprise."

"Can't wait."

"Want me to tell you?" Pierre asked, jumping up and down with excitement.

"You just said it was a surprise."

"A clue, then?" he pleaded.

"Sure."

"Vivaldi."

"A-minor," she guessed correctly.

"Now it's not a surprise," Pierre said, looking a bit regretful.

"Well, you started it. How are the 'threes' going?" Mrs. Kimbrough asked, grinning.

"Not too good. It's a lot harder than I thought."

His mom sat on his bed staring out the window, her shoulders rounded over. And Pierre felt terrible that she didn't have a clue what they were talking about. He made a mental note to try and remember not to get excited about anything in front of his mom. She couldn't take it when people were happy.

As they prepared to leave the house, Mrs. Kimbrough grabbed a grocery sack filled with sandwiches, fruit, and drinks she'd brought along for the trip. Pierre now worried it was obvious that he was glad, even relieved, that Mrs. Kimbrough was coming with them to the hospital. He'd try to remember this also, to downplay that he liked Mrs. Kimbrough so much. That would probably make his mom sad, too.

They piled into Mrs. Kimbrough's car and got on the road for the hour-long drive. The women talked softly in the front seat while Pierre bit into an apple and stuck his nose in the *Nobody* book, which was filled with weirdos. Everyone acted fussy and worried constantly about pretty much nothing. They wrote letters to each other and carried walking sticks and wore tall hats and planned lots of parties where feelings got hurt. People usually loved the wrong person. Most were a little crazy. Some were rich and mean. And, at some point, everybody was sad. Now Pierre's stomach began to ache, probably because reading in the car made him queasy. No, he was thinking way too much about how his mom was sad and how he couldn't fix it. He looked up just as his mom turned down the sun shield to check her makeup in the mirror. Their eyes met in the reflection and she gave him a thumbs-up. Pierre nodded vigorously. But she didn't smile. He lay across the backseat and closed his eyes.

The women gossiped about somebody named Doug who was arrested for kicking his dog. The guy was released, but the dog had to go to the vet. That wasn't fair. Pierre hated Doug, whoever he was, and worried for the dog. Mr. Kimbrough's back was acting up and he had to go to a really expensive chiropractor that they couldn't afford. Pierre became concerned

that the Kimbroughs might not have enough money to eat, and now regretted throwing out the Ringleader's food. He should have offered it to
his teacher. His dad had a bad corn on his toe and went to the foot doctor
to have it sliced off. Pierre hoped that corns weren't contagious, because
what if his mom got the corn? Pierre couldn't fix that, either. In spite of all
Pierre's concerns, his mom just laughed and laughed and laughed, which
didn't make sense, because nothing about their conversation had been
funny. It was all worrisome and unfixable. Pierre's stomachache turned
into a sharp pain. He held his breath and pressed his fists into his belly.

"Listen, Celine, Jim isn't playing the concert tonight in Portland. His
back," Mrs. Kimbrough said. "The chiropractor advised him to lie low for
a couple days. Would you mind if Pierre came with me?"

Mrs. Kimbrough turned to see if he was listening. Ignoring his stomach, Pierre quickly sat up. "Mom, I want to. Can I?" he pleaded.

"How late does it go?" his mom asked.

"Why does that matter? It's summer!" Pierre yelled into the back of
his mom's head.

"That's the thing," Mrs. Kimbrough inserted quickly. "It's an early
outdoor pops concert so we'll be done by eight. Back by ten at the latest. It gets so dark closer to Oslo, and Jim always drives. I could use the
company."

She looked back again and winked at Pierre. His mom agreed easily.
For the rest of the trip, Pierre stared out the window counting gophers on
the interstate. Somehow, he'd remembered this was a rule his dad made
up: when you counted gophers in the car, you weren't allowed to talk.
The women seemed to take his cue and Pierre was grateful for the quiet;
he needed a break from hearing about the many things he couldn't fix.

The tests went quickly, one right after the other. While lying very
still as the machines passed over first his head and then his entire body,
Pierre heard the women try to discuss his condition with the technicians.

As usual, they wouldn't answer any questions. When he gave blood for the millionth time, Pierre complained that he was sick of getting poked. The nurse gave him a strange smile and Pierre figured she actually liked torturing people, because she'd picked a job where she got paid to stick people with needles. Mrs. Kimbrough asked about the medications he was taking, like the pill to prevent brain clots. Pierre had secretly stopped taking that pill because it made him feel worse than he already did. A drug to fix something that wasn't even a problem yet, but made you feel like crap in the meantime, was the dumbest idea ever. All that went fast enough, but then they had to wait over an hour for the theory-of-*nothing* doctor to show up.

"Pierre, tell me how you're doing. In your own words," his doctor demanded in a really loud voice. Pierre wondered whose words he would use other than his own, and why was the guy yelling?

"I feel hopeful," Pierre replied, purposefully vague.

"Have you regained memory at all?"

"I can repeat what you just said."

"I mean longer than a few seconds. For instance, what did you have for breakfast two days ago?"

"Cereal. Whole-wheat toast with honey on top. Glass of orange juice," Pierre recited like an automaton, moving his arms up and down.

"Good. Sounds like progress," the doctor declared, looking around the room for confirmation. Mrs. Kimbrough smiled. His mom nodded. What nobody knew, including his mom because she slept till noon most days, was that Pierre ate the same thing for breakfast every single morning.

"Oh my God. Can we *please* go now?" Pierre whined, rolling his eyes.

"He's cranky today," his mom explained.

"That's not true. I only got cranky when I had to answer his stupid questions."

"That's fine, Pierre. I know this is difficult," the doctor said.

"I didn't say it was difficult. I said it was stupid. Doesn't anybody ever listen!?"

They ate the food Mrs. Kimbrough brought during the first ten minutes of the trip home. His mom only picked at her sandwich and handed the rest to Pierre, which he gladly accepted. Food seemed to relieve his stomach pain, and for the first time in hours he felt decent.

"Well, *he's* a major drip," Mrs. Kimbrough said, stuffing the food wrappers into her canvas bag.

"Yeah, Claude can't stand him," his mom said.

"At least there's *some* people who agree with me about that guy," Pierre said.

"Just because Sandra says Dr. Stanton's a drip and Daddy doesn't like him doesn't mean he's a bad doctor, honey. He's the best in his field," his mom said.

"Tomorrow for breakfast? I want an omelet," Pierre declared.

"You hate eggs," his mom said.

"I know, except once, when I had that omelet with onions. Remember?"

"Oh, right. Daddy made breakfast and there wasn't much in the refrigerator except eggs and onions. But he didn't bother to sauté them. Just threw them in raw. Somehow that made the eggs taste good to you. That was, what, two years ago?"

His mom would never notice, but Mrs. Kimbrough turned around. Pierre avoided her stare and looked out the side window. She rechecked the road, a straightaway, then turned again, this time with a question in her eyes. Mrs. Kimbrough *had* noticed, and Pierre didn't look away.

It started the week before. Like remembering that Ben *was* his friend and that Ben's mom and dad were divorced, and they ate pizza every night for dinner because his dad didn't give them enough money. And that Edna's daughter was dead, and that she'd been Luc's mother. Small things, weird stuff, all useless. Because what good did it do him to remember a fight from months ago when his dad forgot to change the oil in his mom's car? And what was so great about remembering raw onions in an omelet? Pretty much nothing.

Everyone was obsessed with the past. If it was bad, they were glad it was over. If it was good, they wanted to repeat it. And thinking about the future made even less sense. His mom and dad and the theory doctor, and *even* Mrs. Kimbrough, all wanted to know what was going to happen. Pierre knew this was impossible. There was only *now,* like when he played his violin. And right now, everyone in the car was ignoring the fact that before leaving the hospital, when his mom made a point of going to the restroom alone, she'd taken a pill. Pierre saw it and he knew Mrs. Kimbrough noticed, too. You only had to listen to her sloppy talk to prove it.

"Tonight, stay on the interstate as long as you can, Sandra," his mom advised, slowly bobbing her head up and down.

"Of course," she agreed.

"What'll you do then, loop around the lake? Cause that's the fastest way."

"I suppose . . ."

"And it could rain later. So, you might want to take the longer route—"

Pierre bolted forward and *Nobody* flew to the floor of the car. "Shut up, Mom!" he yelled.

"I'm trying to figure out the route for Sandra . . ." Her voice trailed off.

"She doesn't *need* your help. And you don't even know what you're talking about," Pierre whimpered.

"I certainly know how to drive to Portland," she said, scratching her scalp and inspecting the dandruff, another sign of her pills.

"But don't you see, Mom? You can't help with something in the future. There's no *point* to it," Pierre said with desperation.

"*Hey*. Take it easy, Pierre," Mrs. Kimbrough said.

"No, Sandra. He's right. There's no point," his mom said with a strange flatness.

Before his mom could start to cry, because that's what she always did, Pierre wrapped his arms around her from the backseat and squeezed as hard as he could. She still smelled like the shower she'd taken that morning.

"Don't cry, Mom. Everything's going to be okay. Nothing will happen," Pierre whispered into her hair.

LYING LIARS

"WHAT WAS YOUR FAVORITE PART?" SANDRA asked Pierre. She reached behind her seat in the car and felt for her violin in the footwell, to make certain it was secure for the drive home. Pierre tossed his book onto the dashboard and buckled his seat belt.

"The violin," Pierre said.

"You mean the soloist?"

"Uh-huh," Pierre affirmed without enthusiasm.

Since she'd brought him backstage after the concert to introduce him to a few of her colleagues, Pierre had gradually slipped into a sullen mood. Though loquacious one-on-one, she knew Pierre was typically shy in groups, and so she simply assumed he'd been overwhelmed by the attention he'd received as Sandra's prize student. Now, as he stared out the window toward the outdoor pavilion where the orchestra had just finished performing, Sandra examined Pierre's profile. Eyes blinking rapidly, his mouth grimacing with thought, fingers thrumming his thighs. She reached over and tucked a few longish strands of hair behind his ear, apparently remaining a beat too long, as Pierre sloughed off her gesture with his shoulder and sidled closer to the side window. Then he pulled his book off the dashboard and buried his nose.

"Book any good?" she asked, hoping to drag something out of him. Pierre gave her a tired stare, as if to say, *I'm reading now.*

"All righty, then," she said with jocularity. "Let's get on the road."

Sandra circled toward the exit of the municipal parking lot. At intervals, she waved goodbye to friends, most of whom called out to Pierre, "Keep practicing!" Each time, Pierre produced a weak smile, only to resume his book and disposition. Sandra knew how to avoid post-concert traffic and navigated the back roads of Portland, then slid onto the interstate heading north. Within minutes of gaining speed on a long straightaway, Pierre let the book slip to his lap. His head lolled back and in no time, his eyelids dropped.

It was a few minutes after eight, yet the sun still beat with force from the west. Sandra was grateful that the concert was over early, because the long day had all but exhausted her. Pierre now looked to have fallen deeply asleep, and she surmised that the stress of testing at the hospital had finally gotten the better of him, too. A parade of practitioners had methodically interrogated and prodded him, each one asking virtually the same questions as the previous. Then the final consult with Stanton, whose vacuous personality did next to nothing to either enlighten or reassure them. The frustration level was more than any adult could manage, let alone a boy. Yet Sandra, who'd attended a fair number of these appointments, admired Pierre's wily people skills. Such as placating Stanton with good-enough answers to his obtuse questions, while at the same time deftly sidestepping more treacherous queries with the prattle of an innocent. With the exception of his final meltdown during the drive home (and she could hardly blame the boy), Sandra thought she understood Pierre's ulterior motive: to appear as normal as possible so he might protect his mother.

Claude, had he been there, would have been pleased with Pierre's shenanigans—like father, like son. Celine, on the other hand, was oblivious not only to Pierre's high-wire act, but her own presentation as well. The morning had begun optimistically enough; they'd had fun styling her hair, applying makeup, and choosing just the right outfit. For some reason, Celine felt it important to appear virginal. She'd dressed so primly— a getup with buttons to her neck, sleeves below her wrists, and a hemline reaching mid-calf—she looked like an ex-nun who hadn't quite embraced the good life. But no amount of Vatican camp could mitigate her battered stare. Below her eyes, where exhaustion and sadness coalesced, a stack of dark bags were evidence enough that if anyone looked more than three times, Celine would have been suspected of some degree of drug use. Which made Pierre's ability to nuance the absurdities of the morning all the more admirable. He dealt every authority figure a full deck of three-card-monte misdirection. Sandra now glanced at Pierre, his chin stuck to his chest, his pug nose snuffling in fits, very much just a boy. Few adults could have pulled off a sleight of hand such as Pierre had that morning.

Daylight suddenly vacated the sky, the way it seemed to do only in Maine. Sandra flicked on the headlights and noticed that while she'd been absorbed in thought, her speed had dipped below the limit. A few cars sped past her on the right, honking to encourage a move to the slow lane. Instead, she stepped on the gas and Pierre jolted awake, rubbing his eyes.

"Are we home?"

"No, it's only been about ten minutes," she said.

He reached into his pocket and pulled out a few nuts left over from earlier in the day. "I'm hungry. Can we stop somewhere to eat?"

"We shouldn't. I told your mom we'd be back by ten. But I think there's an apple in my bag on the backseat."

"I'll wait," Pierre snapped.

"Did you like the piece the soloist played?"

"Yeah."

"It's from a movie called *Schindler's List.*"

"I *know*. I read it in the program."

"What's the matter?" she asked.

"Nothing."

"Okay. What else did you like?"

"I can't remember. *Remember?*"

"Sweetie—"

"I'm not *your* sweetie. I'm supposed to be my mom's sweetie. Except now she's calling me honey . . . ," he said, his voice shaking.

She felt Pierre's stare fixed on her face, expecting either sympathy or admonishment, maybe both. Then it struck Sandra; he was testing her. Pierre was trying very hard to collapse, and where, but with her, could that happen? His parents had given him no such space.

"Tell me," she demanded.

"Tell you what?"

"What's got you so upset?"

He shook his head vigorously, red hair flopping about.

"Is it about the concert?"

"No."

"Something about this morning at the hospital?"

"Not really."

"The Ringleader?"

"Yuck. No!"

"Look," she said with some frustration. "I can feed you a hundred questions. Or you can just tell me."

"It's *you.*"

"*Me?*" She couldn't help but spit out a laugh.

"It's not funny. I'm mad at you."

"*Why?*" she asked, incredulous.

MARCIA BUTLER

"Wait. I'm sorry. I didn't mean it . . . ," Pierre said, backtracking.

"No, no, Pierre. Keep going. I can take it," she said.

Pierre sighed like an ancient man. "You're starting to act like my parents."

"*What?*" This not only shocked Sandra, but she was ashamed to admit that she was offended. "In what way?"

"You're not being honest."

Now she felt herself getting really defensive. "About what? How've I lied to you?"

"It's not lying, not exactly. It's more like . . ." Pierre paused and seemed to be considering his words carefully. Maybe he'd picked up on her sensitivity. Sandra, now thoroughly disgusted with herself, wondered who the adult was.

"My parents won't talk," he finally began. "They go around all day not talking about anything. No matter what happens, they don't talk about it. And it's really, really weird. But I know I'm the reason, so I guess I shouldn't complain—"

"Okay, hold up a minute," she interrupted. "I'm getting that you wish your parents would talk. And that you think it's your fault. Which, by the way, it absolutely is *not*. But how am I like them? Because we talked nonstop on the ride up."

"Yeah, we talked. But not about the most important *thing*." Pierre crossed his arms in defeat, as if he had no faith that she could ever guess what it was he needed.

"Just say it, Pierre. I really don't know what you're upset about. What's this important thing?"

He continued to sit very still, embedded in his frustration.

"Look," she said. "Sometimes you have to help adults—we're sort of dumb, you know."

He seemed to like this notion, the dumb part, because she detected

138

a chuckle.

"I've gotten some memory back. You noticed it on the ride home from the hospital. I saw it in your face. You had the whole trip to Portland to ask me about it. But you didn't. *And I was waiting,*" he said, whispering the last sentence, almost ashamed.

Sandra saw a ramp to a service area coming up in a quarter mile. "Let's get you something to eat. I'm pretty hungry too."

They snaked into a Wendy's drive-through, ordered chicken sandwiches and Cokes, and got back on the highway. While they ate, they chatted more about the concert, and she answered his questions about what it was like to play in an orchestra. All the while, Pierre blotted her chin of any sauce dribbles as she drove. And he behaved as if satisfied with the way things stood: that he hadn't necessarily needed an answer, rather only to voice an injustice. How she'd hurt him. Which deeply saddened Sandra, because she then realized that Pierre didn't actually expect that anything would change. Such a reasonable outcome, especially with regard to the adults in his life, was not part of his current daily experience.

"I did notice that you were remembering. And I've been very excited about it. But I didn't want to pressure you, so I suppose that's why I didn't say anything. I was waiting for you, and if that was a mistake on my part, I apologize."

"It's fine. I'm over it," Pierre quipped with finality. He crumpled all the sandwich wrappings and empty cups into a wad, stuffed them in the Wendy's bag, and tossed it into the backseat. Then he switched on the radio and tried to pick up any station that could break through mountain interference. After zeroing in on an all-sports talk station, which she knew held no interest for either of them, Sandra brushed his hand away to turn off the dial.

"Okay, here's what I think," she continued. "You're exactly right. When I noticed you'd remembered, I should have said something. If not then and there, then yes, on the ride to Portland. That was very, very wrong of me."

"It's okay, Mrs. Kimbrough. *Really*."

Again, he accepted her rephrased and more direct apology with his usual good nature. Yet all the subtext remained unspoken. What did the recovered memories mean to him? And who would be his sounding board to work this through? Not his doctors, certainly. Clearly, not his parents. Sandra wanted to be that one and only person. But, as Pierre had pointed out, she wasn't so very different from Celine and Claude after all.

"Look!" Pierre cried. "The deer eyes."

Indeed, families had gathered on the roadside, their phosphorescent eyes glowing.

"Better than the gophers from this morning, right?" she noted.

"They were cute," Pierre defended.

"I suppose."

"Mrs. Kimbrough, there's something I can't get out of my head," he said.

"Gophers?"

"No, nothing like that. Something much weirder."

"Gophers are pretty weird."

"No jokes!"

Once again, she was failing this boy's heart. "Tell me."

"Memory. It's not working for me."

"Your photos and papers? Your method?"

"I gave that up a while ago," he said with a brush of his hand.

"But it was so great—"

"It was stupid."

"Why stupid?"

"Because when I used the method and *did* remember things, almost all of the memories were about stuff that I didn't really care about. It was all busywork and useless. Because there's nothing you can do about the past. And the future's exactly the same. So why even bother? See, that's what I figured out. I don't want to remember anything, and I don't want to worry about what's going to happen next. All it does is make you nervous. And sad."

On any other day, with any other person, Sandra would have argued his point as if defending *Roe v. Wade* in the Supreme Court. But Pierre had landed on the essence of something so obvious: every person she knew, including herself, *was* sad. At times, intolerably so. Preoccupation with the past and future seemed to do that to people. There was no possible rebuttal to his beautiful logic.

"I can't say I disagree."

"You *don't*?" he asked, surprised.

"No. What you say is true. The past and the future are just ideas, or constructs."

"Constructs? What's that?"

"It's a bit complicated to explain, but let me put it another way. One of the reasons I like to play the violin is because music isn't in the past or the future. It's right now. And it's okay to feel the sadness in music, because in the very next phrase there's joy. Plus, lots and lots of other emotions in between. Everything's very immediate in music, and I bet that's one of the reasons you like playing violin so much, too. We're lucky that way, Pierre."

"Maybe . . ."

The exit merging onto the county road heading toward Oslo appeared. Sandra immediately engaged the high beams, as she now drove in pitch dark. For a novice to the area, the brake pedal would have been overused. But Sandra slid into turns with ease and plenty of gas. And they were at a higher elevation now, so the next leg of the trip would yield good radio reception.

"You can get something now," she said. "Try 98.7."

Pierre dialed it in. They caught the end of the Boston Pops concert at Hatch Shell on the Charles River Esplanade, just as all hell was breaking loose with the conclusion of the 1812 Overture. It was one of the first CDs Sandra had given to Pierre, and he'd gotten hooked on Tchaikovsky's bombast. They sang along, Sandra on the violin part—no easy feat—and Pierre with melodies from the brass and winds. There was something heroic and uplifting about their voices saturating the interior of the car. Almost as confirmation that music itself could compel two people driving in a car to sing louder and louder, trying to obliterate the orchestra. Trying to grab the joy. Then, Pierre dropped out, leaving Sandra's voice wailing with an abandon worthy of an embarrassing karaoke moment. He held his stomach, gasping with laughter.

"That's not fair!" Sandra cried, also laughing at herself. "You have a much better voice. *And* perfect pitch—"

Suddenly Pierre was thrown into her lap and then just as quickly landed back in his seat. The car whirled to the left and she immediately corrected out of instinct. Then it slammed the other way, so she pumped the brakes, which caused a hard shudder. Pierre braced his arms against the dashboard, then swung back and reached behind to grab on to the headrest. His only sound was: "Whooooa!" Sandra felt her body decompensate. Sweat poured out. Her hands slipped off the steering wheel, her arms like limp noodles. A queasy fear caused her belly to do a roller-coaster drop. For some reason, her nose filled and started to drip. Then, as the 1812 Overture was concluding with cymbal crashes and chiming bells, safety-glass pellets from the back windshield flew around the inside of the car. All of this happened within a few seconds, and she could only ride it out while listening to fireworks miles away in Boston until the car came to a stop.

Pierre immediately turned the radio off and the sudden silence felt a relief. The only sound was the engine pinging as it normally did after a long drive.

"I think we hit something," he offered tentatively.

"Are you okay?" she asked, grabbing his hand. "You didn't buckle your seat belt when we left the Wendy's."

"It doesn't matter now. I'm fine."

She twisted the key to the battery position and switched on the inside roof light and headlights.

"Your nose is bloody," he said, dabbing at Sandra's upper lip to show her.

She smeared the blood off with her fingers and wiped it on her black concert pants. Fingertip callouses on her left hand had grabbed the burgundy color and she remembered her violin. Sandra quickly pulled it to the front and found it intact. *Thank God*, she thought to herself. Their instruments, aside from the land, were the only material things she and Jim owned of any value.

"Stay where you are, Pierre. I'll see what's happened."

The car stood at an angle across the road span. Pellets of glass from the back windshield crunched as she walked around the car a few times. Then she noticed some thin trees broken at the side of the road, literally bent just above the roots. That's when she saw an animal's rump a few feet down a shallow embankment. She approached tentatively and poked her toe into its back end to see if it was alive. The animal yielded to the pressure without otherwise moving. She pushed harder and held the pressure, this time with the entire sole of her shoe. Not a twitch. Sandra knelt down, placed her hand on its still-hot rump, and ran her fingers down a long back leg. She pulled her phone out of a sweater pocket and with the aid of the flashlight, was able to make out distinctive scarring on the animal's flank. She gasped to herself. "Oh no, *please no*." The fact that she could exactly identify this moose pained Sandra, and the adrenalin of fear now rushed through her body. Pierre had become attached to this moose, as it often came around when he took his lessons.

Sandra left the moose and began to inspect Pierre's side of the car more closely, which had suffered the most damage. The rearview mirror had been sliced off, and she noticed tufts of fur caught on some of the metal detailing. But other than a dented back door and the missing wind-shield, the damage was miraculously minimal, most likely because of the size of their ancient Oldsmobile sedan. That Jim had stubbornly refused to part with it all these years probably saved their lives that night. She got back in the car and turned off the lights.

"What is it?" Pierre asked.

"A deer. The good news is it's dead, so it won't suffer."

Her call to Jim went unanswered, which wasn't a surprise, because he didn't believe in the current trend of availability at all times of the day or night. She tried a few times in succession as a signal for him to pick up, which he didn't. She figured he must be in the tub soaking his back. Either that or he'd taken a pill and was asleep. Not wanting to alarm him, she left a voice message that they'd been in a small accident and would be home soon. But now her mind raced ahead, realizing that she also needed to call in the incident to the police. As much as she didn't want to think of it this way, the dead moose was a windfall. With an official claim on the animal, she and Jim could live for a year on the meat, and they needed it as badly as anyone in Oslo. She looked at Pierre as he examined some glass pellets he'd scooped up from the backseat. He'd been unusually quiet, and Sandra wondered if his calm was a kind of shock. She'd wait till later to call the cops.

"They're kind of pretty. Like jewels. Don't you think?" he said, displaying them with both hands.

"Yes, they sparkle. Can you buckle up, please? I'll see if I can drive this old hog."

She turned over the ignition and the engine engaged after a few sputters. The car shook a bit but settled down once she gave it more gas. They proceeded toward Oslo at a surprisingly good speed. Shortly, they came to a fork, one path circling the lake, the other leading toward Sandra's house, still at least fifteen minutes away. But then she saw Edna's house across the black water, lights blazing from the first floor.

"Pierre, I have an idea. Let's go to Edna's. It's just a few minutes from here, and I want to make certain you're okay."

"Sure. But there's only a few scratches from the glass bits," he said, displaying his forearms.

"I'm worried about the car, too. It's pretty old, and those steep hills closer to our houses might be a problem. Anyway, it'll be safer this way."

HER CALF HAD finally been able to rise, so the moose would now make her pilgrimage. She approached the white-furred female's area. There, she'd observed things that were not typical of other humans. Such as the female's mate sitting on top of their structure. She heard noises from inside, something like birds. These songs continued day after day. She roamed there for several hours, circling their structure, breathing in the white-furred female's violet odor, which the moose had come to associate with safety. This had been a place where she could eat and rest with little fear.

The other area, though still dangerous, was also necessary to revisit. She climbed up and over the mountain, where she then saw the massive structure that made a foul wind. She passed the spot where the snake had prevented her from moving. Where she could not drink water. Where her calf had become quiet inside her. Where humans dragged her to a place of no sky and no earth and no horizon. Where she'd smelled a past of torture and death. Where she'd listened to the risen-animal world call with warnings. And where, to be free and save her unborn calf, she had inflicted

·damage and pain on the small human with red fur.

Night had come and the moose, having completed her pilgrimage, now roamed on the path around the large water. She heard a grinding noise in the distance. She turned to look up the hill and saw a long metal container. It sped faster as it approached. Closer. The sound grew in her ears. Closer. She gathered her legs. Closer. Now she ran. Ran as never before. Ran from the natural world. Ran from all dangers. Ran toward her dead calf. Now. The moose met the long metal container. Now. The moose rose. *Now*.

PARANOIA IS KNOWING ALL THE FACTS

ONCE THEY'D RETURNED FROM THE hospital, and with Sandra due back within the hour to pick up Pierre, Celine gathered some energy and set to fixing him a quick meal. She watched her son munch on a hamburger with onion and tomato, a dab of honey mustard. At one point he stopped chewing mid-motion and offered her half. Celine smiled and shook her head, chagrined by his vigilant scrutiny. Pierre doted on her in so many ways. Like making sure she drank enough water, especially when she didn't eat. Shyly suggesting that she apply deodorant before they leave the house. Brushing the snarled hair at the back of her head, which she'd often neglect. And giving her hard hugs, telling her that he'd be okay when she knew full well that *nothing,* in any way, was okay. But she'd nod, needing to believe in her son's naïve optimism. Not only was Celine siphoning off Pierre's good nature, but she'd begun to see herself as one of those opportunistic ocean feeders, like the fish that attached themselves to the bottom of a shark for a meal or a ride. As she'd done with Claude. Even as he chided her, threatened her, pitied her, Celine still counted on Claude's stalwart love and his willingness to always grant affection on request. And the empirical fact that Sandra enriched Pierre's life more than she ever could was a sure sign that, however perverse, Sandra was the best person Celine had ever known.

She stood on the steps to her house and watched them drive off to the concert, something Celine had no understanding of. Pierre's squeals of happiness unfurled through the open window. Their heads bobbed up and down, turned side to side—chatting, agreeing, enjoying. That Sandra was preparing her son for his future was clear enough. But in her dark imagination, Celine saw a scenario where they'd not return. Perhaps not on this particular night, but eventually Sandra would take Pierre and give him the life his talent deserved. And Celine knew that once Pierre stopped missing Claude and especially her, he'd be fine. Really, so much better off. She couldn't, at this moment, predict the emotional land mines sure to come from such an abduction. But surely everyone would come to appreciate the wisdom of this eventuality. Because if you loved Pierre Roy, if you understood his needs, if you cared at all about his happiness, well, Sandra was the best solution.

Celine sat at her kitchen table and gripped her midsection. This potential conclusion had produced the exact same pain—a drill digging a hole in her belly—as when she'd discovered Pierre was in the hospital from an accident that no one could, or would, explain to her. She knew of only two methods of relief and chose the one closest to her. She reached for the landline sitting across from her on the table and dialed Jim.

Eight, nine, ten rings . . .

She plunked the handset on the table and stared at the sound. He was there. She knew it. Where else could he be, what with the back pain that Sandra said prevented him from playing the concert that evening? Now her legs ached, her head itched, her fingers twitched. She went clammy cold. Pierre had placed a shawl on the back rung of her chair before he left. *In case you need it, Mom.* Despite the summer heat, she wrapped herself inside the wool, once again sad that her son had learned to antici-pate her discomfort. That was *her* job. But she couldn't even remember whether Pierre had taken his jacket for the evening chill. And truly, what kind of mother summoned her best efforts for the likes of Dr. Stanton? Because he was *specifically* who she'd stayed straight for earlier in the day. Not for her son. And now Celine wanted that second remedy: a pill.

Eighteen, nineteen, twenty rings . . .

Why would Jim torture her like this? They didn't fight. No couple-like conflicts resulting in resentment and brooding. The worst thing might be one bringing Chinese food when the other preferred deli sandwiches. Or who went down on whom, first. And nothing was off-limits. Jim was amenable to every position, endless topics, and most importantly, all of her faults. That is, until she'd broken one lousy rule the day after Pierre's accident and called him. Jesus, her son had been hurt! But since that day, Celine interpreted every eyebrow twitch as an indication of cracks in their fuselage. *My eyebrows are innocent bystanders!* was how Jim typically reas-sured her. Now Celine imagined Jim sitting in his house, staring at her incoming number, waiting her out. Hoping she'd give up and maybe even disappear from his life altogether.

Twenty-nine, thirty, thirty-one . . .

The phone went dead. Celine slumped. Then within five seconds, her cell buzzed from across the room.

"Don't ever call me on the landline," Jim said, his voice quiet and harsh.

"I thought it'd be harder to trace—"

"*No.* It's all listed, including date and time. Sandra pays the bills. She practically uses a microscope. Have I made my *point*?" he said, now almost breathless.

"But now the cell. How do we fix that?"

"I can't believe we're having this conversation. What the fuck is wrong with you?"

Claude had also used that phrase when, the previous night, she'd demanded another pair of Jimmy Choos. *You've already got five pairs. What the fuck's wrong with you?* Both men in her life asking the same rhetorical question, the answer so blatantly obvious. What the fuck, indeed. She walked to the bathroom with the cell clamped between her shoulder and ear and took the bottle down from the top shelf.

"Meet me?" she whimpered, sitting on the toilet.

"What for?"

"I wouldn't ask unless it was urgent."

"I don't think so."

"*Please.*"

Jim didn't answer. A fresh unease filtered through her body. She cupped some water from the faucet and tipped it into her mouth, then smeared the remainder on her face. The liquid had mixed with her dried sweat. She tasted salt, which roiled her stomach slightly.

"Does this have to do with Pierre's appointment?" he finally asked. "Sandra didn't say much—she was in and out."

Now she latched on like a grifter—his concern for her son.

"In a way," she said, though it wasn't anything about Pierre. More that the pain in her stomach now felt terminal. "You know she took Pierre with her to Portland?"

"No."

"Well, they're tied up for hours and Claude's at his shift. Meet me."

"Can't do it," he said with a sigh.

"Jim—"

"*Stop it.* Anyway, I was in bed, which is where I'm headed to now. Bye."

The pill Celine was thinking about swallowing sat clamped in her hand. Sweat had caused a slight melt, and the residue was settling into her life crease. She blew on the pill and dropped it into her dress pocket, then rinsed her palm. After slipping into sturdy shoes, she threw off the shawl and left the house.

The summer heat was still intense despite it being six p.m. But a canopy of pine trees along the road buffered the sun, making it feel at least ten degrees cooler. With an intermittent breeze, walking actually felt a comfort. And surprisingly, her legs, whose calf muscles had greatly weakened from weeks of oversleeping and lack of exercise, were strong enough to propel her up the steep incline on the road common to the two properties. In short order, she passed the abandoned campground, shut down a year earlier. In spite of its close proximity, Claude had always forbidden Pierre to attend such a place. *No son of his* . . . Celine agreed, though mostly because Pierre had always been solitary. And truth be told, she couldn't imagine him enjoying days on end with a bunch of nose-picking boys.

After cresting the hill, Celine headed into an open field, where she happened upon the remnants of a bonfire. Field stones and rocks, with tall summer grasses thriving in between, circled charred logs. Wands meant for marshmallow roasting lay scattered about, and faded *Highlights* magazines were stuck together from what looked like many seasons of snow and rain. She wasn't sure whose land she was standing on at the moment, Kimbrough or Roy. Claude hadn't been *that* obnoxious as to red-stake the boundary so near to where they all lived. In any case, the fire pit was completely out of view from both the road and their houses. Celine, turning in circles to get her bearings, was suddenly disoriented—almost frightened. She probed the pill in her pocket. Just then the sun vanished behind a low bank of clouds, which caused the lights at Jim's house to appear. Relieved, she withdrew her hand, chiding herself for her paranoia.

As with every mirage, the final leg of the walk took longer than she expected, perhaps another ten minutes. And having not eaten since the ride home from the hospital, she was by now very hungry. She approached at the back of the house and, standing outside the sliding glass doors, stared into the kitchen. Music blared. "Josie" by Steely Dan. Jim, bare-chested and wearing only his boxer shorts, ran on a treadmill at high speed. His arms pumped in sync with his gait, like a stallion in its prime. Sweat trickled down his torso and flew off his hair. Then the song changed to "Layla." After turning off the treadmill, Jim jumped to the floor and tossed off about fifty push-ups without pausing. He segued into sit-ups, squeezing his eyes shut with the effort. Celine watched, bewildered by the ease with which he exercised. Jim had back problems.

Knocking didn't cut through Eric Clapton, so she slid open the door, walked over to Jim, and nudged his foot with the toe of her shoe.

"What the *hell*!" he yelled, and crab-walked back before collapsing.

"The door was open," Celine explained sheepishly.

Jim reached behind him to shut off the music. He took a towel from the kitchen counter and wiped his neck and chest, then dropped a Grateful Dead T-shirt over his head.

"*What?*" he asked, arms crossed, foot tapping.

"What about your back?" she asked, pointing to the treadmill.

"What about it?" he said, like a sixteen-year-old sassing his least favorite parent. "Give me your phone."

"I didn't bring it," she said, patting her dress pockets to make sure.

"Wonderful." Jim smirked. "Delete that call when you go home. It's still in the cloud, but it'll have to do."

She nodded, produced a broad smile and took his hand.

"Not so fast," he said, retracting from her as if burned. "Celine. *Seriously?*"

"I need you."

"You get every conceivable part of me twice a month."

"I didn't mean it like *that*," she said with a wounded look.

"Neither did I."

They stared at each other for a few seconds until he yielded.

"Oh Jesus, sit down. You look terrible."

"I'm hungry."

Jim went to the refrigerator, removed a jug of chilled water, and poured them two glasses. He grabbed a container of hummus, a couple of carrots, pita bread, and laid plates and silverware opposite each other. "This is all I've got. We're a bit low on groceries at the moment."

While Celine devoured most of the food and several glasses of water, Jim ate very little. A bowl of M&M's sat between them, which he pecked at. When she finished, Jim scooped a handful and flicked several her way. Every sound in the large room was amplified, including her jaw crunching on the candy. The bright clatter of plates, the bang of their glasses on the stone tabletop. Chairs scraping on the floor as they occasionally repositioned themselves. Shrill. They'd never shared a meal anywhere but the Loon, where most noise, human or otherwise, was absorbed by the stained carpet and dreary upholstery. This kitchen, with all its bouncy surfaces, was without a doubt Sandra's territory. And Celine felt like she'd traveled not just down the road but to a far-off country whose language she'd never master and culture she'd never assimilate into. Forever the "other."

"When's the last time you were here?" Jim asked as if reading her mind.

"I've avoided it since we started. I really can't remember."

"Well, with Claude's Maine snobbery and now you and me, the four of us have never been the easiest of neighbors. Though Sandra's tried pretty damned hard."

"Sandra's a good person," Celine said.

"That she is," Jim concurred, nodding slowly. "Couldn't live without her."

"Me neither," Celine agreed quickly, surprised by her own admission.

The food and water had satisfied, and at last Celine's body settled into some degree of normal. She sat back on her chair and stretched out her legs, appreciating a fullness to her belly. The ache had lessened well enough. They stayed quiet now, which Celine was grateful for, because at this moment she wasn't nearly as desperate as when she'd left her house. She even understood why Jim hung up on her, and was about to suggest that they forget the whole episode. Just give him a kiss on the cheek and rewind the clock as if this had never happened.

At least that was the plan, until Jim dropped his head to the table and began to weep. Celine stretched her arms out and they gripped each other's hands. She held tight, didn't move a muscle—her restraint to not ask questions, a miracle. All so Jim could stay with whatever was making him hurt so, just as he'd done for her on too many occasions.

Jim pressed his palms to his eyes, wiping tears. "There's nothing wrong with my back," he whispered.

"That's obvious. I watched you work out like an iron man before I came in."

"You were spying?" He sniffed indignantly.

"Not spying, just waiting for you to finish. But I *was* surprised."

"Don't you want to know why?"

"Of course." Celine took a sip of water and shoved the glass to him. He drank deeply.

"I've been faking the pain to get out of concerts."

"What? That doesn't make sense. *Why?*"

"It's complicated. But as long as I keep going to the chiropractor he'll sign off on no playing, and I can take my sick days and still get paid."

"Can't they tell? I mean that you're faking it."

"Hell no. All you have to do is say you're in agony. What can they do, accuse me of lying? Why would anyone lie about pain? Well, I guess there's lots of reasons. But it's good for them, too. They get to prescribe another batch of sessions. What a scam."

"But why get out of concerts?"

"Oh Jesus." Jim took the bottom of his T-shirt and wiped his face of sweat. "How to put this. I don't want to play the cello anymore. I've had it. I'm overwhelmed. Exhausted. I hate the whole damned profession."

"You don't mean that."

"I'd love it if somebody'd run it over with a truck. Better, steal the damn thing. At least we'd get an insurance claim out of it."

"But you and Sandra are artists—"

"Don't idealize, Celine. You don't know the first thing about it. We don't have an easy or even good life. What we do, driving to kingdom come and back. Scrounging for the odd gig. It's like being a traveling salesman. With terrible sales. And now Sandra's up to her eyeballs with students."

"But why do you have to fake the pain? Can't you tell Sandra any of this?"

"Are you kidding? We're flat broke. The house systems are breaking down. There's no hot water. Neither of us has bought clothes in a couple of years. Sandra's off to Goodwill every month to scrounge. Bottom line, we can't survive unless I bring in my income from the symphony. And we owe a lot of people money. I'm surprised you haven't heard . . . have you?"

"No."

"Not even a whiff from Claude? The town crier?"

"Nothing."

"Whatever. I'm not the first person in the world who hated his job. I'll figure it out."

"I'll lend you money."

"Right. That's the *last* thing you need."

"But we've got it."

Jim shook his head, doubtful. "You guys have got to be as tight as we are."

"Claude's pretty flush."

"What does that mean? Rich?"

"No, not like that. But . . . you know Claude . . ."

"No. What?"

"He's always had some sort of side hustle going. But lately there seems to be more money. Cash. I don't ask."

"That's really nice of you, but it's a terrible idea. And anyway, Sandra would never allow it. But I've been trying to fix the solar panels on my own. There's a flaw in the system and I think I'm onto something pretty cool . . ." Jim's voice disappeared. "*Listen* to me."

She walked around the table and sat in his lap. Jim gathered her in his arms, and she looked into his eyes, all rheumy. They kissed, primly at first with Jim holding back; it was his house, after all. Then he pushed into her and the kiss deepened.

"I think I want to live," Jim said softly into her neck.

"You'd better," she said, now stroking his cheeks.

"Do *you*?" he asked.

"Do I what?"

"Want to live?"

"I haven't taken one since this morning."

She took the pill out of her pocket and placed it on the table. Jim lobbed it into the farmhouse sink. She heard it ping several times against porcelain.

"I guess that's that," she said, laughing. "I'd better get going. Can you zip me down to my house?"

"Sure, but why are we breaking a rule? You never told me."

"Oh. Right. It doesn't seem that important now. Forgive me?"

"Don't I always?" he said while glancing at his cell. "Christ. It's almost nine thirty . . . wait. This is strange. There's a couple hang-ups from Sandra, and a voicemail."

Jim listened for about ten seconds, put the phone down, and cleared his throat.

"What is it? You look strange."

"Aw hell. Sandra's had an accident," he said.

"*Pierre?*"

Jim opened his mouth, then shut it. He nodded.

Celine's hand immediately went to her dress pocket. She dug deep, feeling the creases and seams along the bottom, searching for something small and round. When that yielded nothing, she gripped the fabric, trying to pull the pocket inside out. A few pieces of lint fluttered to the floor. She ran to the sink. It had been freshly rinsed, no dishes stacked, no glasses rimmed with wine. Yes, this was Sandra's domain, and that small round thing had skittered down her drain unimpeded.

Jim came up behind. She turned and buried her face against his chest. She could just make out Jerry Garcia's face on his T-shirt. *Please God, not again.*

NO PLACE FOR ONIONS

EDNA HAD JUST EASED HER SHOES OFF and was massaging her bunions when Sandra's late-afternoon call came. Since Pierre's accident, she had relied on Sandra to share details of Pierre's progress, and so she'd been on needles most of the day, eager to hear about the boy's hospital visit.

"Oh, *good*. It's you. So. How did he do?" Edna asked.

"As far as the testing went, same old same old, but—"

"What's that, Sandra?" Edna pressed her hand over one ear to drown out *Hollywood Squares*, blasting from the family room into the kitchen.

"He's begun to remember."

"*No*! Tell me."

"It was a small thing. He let it slip on the ride home. Celine didn't pick up on it—at least I don't think so. But I did, and I'm pretty sure Pierre noticed."

"You have to be delicate, Sandra."

"Right. I'm taking him to Portland for the pops concert. I'll see if he's ready to talk."

"Maybe you should wait for him to say something first? He's such a private boy."

"That's my instinct, too."

"What about Jim? Will Pierre open up with him there?"

"Jim's off this concert set. His back."

"It's all that *roof* work. Much too difficult."

"Not the roof. Surprisingly, that's about the only thing with the house that's held up," Sandra said. "It's the solar panels. There's some disconnection and as usual, he's convinced he can fix it."

"Well, he *can't*."

"I know, but you can't tell Jim anything he doesn't want to hear. Anyway, he fell halfway down the ladder a while ago and he's been in agony ever since."

"Dear lord, Sandra. Poor man," Edna said, looking at her watch. "Oh *no*. It's *Feud* night and I'm not nearly ready."

"Okay, I've got to run myself. I'm due to pick up Pierre in a few minutes."

"Call me tomorrow?"

"You bet—"

"Hang on, Sandra. How's Celine?" Edna asked.

"Not too bad, actually. A slight blip at the end. I'll fill you in later."

Edna hung up just in time to see the pizza-delivery truck roll up their drive. She ran out to meet the teenager as he approached with two boxes.

"Such a *delay* today, Tony. I hope Leon got it right this time," she said.

"Sorry, Mrs. Sibley, but we got jammed in the last two hours. It says no onions on the order," Tony said, waving the slip of paper in front of her.

"I'll have to take your word for it. I'm in a terrible rush," she said. "Say hello to your mother. Here's a five."

"Thanks, Mrs. Sibley," he said, pocketing the bill.

She returned to the kitchen and immediately opened the boxes. Her heart sank. Onions. They liked different toppings, so she'd typically order two medium pies, one with plain American cheese for Luc, and for her, a collection of vegetables. Edna wouldn't allow meat of any sort on Leon's pizza—their beef was so gristly she could only assume it came from throwaway parts of the animal, such as ears or lips. But the pizza parlor added onions to every order pro forma, and she'd begged Leon to keep them off Luc's pies, explaining how they gave him terrible heartburn, which kept him from sleeping well, which then made him grumpy in the morning and usually led to him having a bad day. Edna stared at the mess of oily onions lying on congealed cheese and chided herself. Why would she expect Leon to remember, let alone care, about Luc's digestive tract and subsequent moods? She took a pair of tongs out of a drawer and began to tweeze off the finely minced onions. But Luc was already in the den finishing up with *Squares* and waiting for his favorite show to begin in just a few minutes, so she abandoned this time-consuming method and began scraping with a fork.

One night each week, Edna suspended the tradition of formal dining and indulged Luc's obsession for the TV program *Family Feud*. He'd discovered an obscure channel showing back-to-back reruns from the 1980s and was devoted to Richard Dawson, the original host during that era. Edna was happy to accommodate anything Luc showed enthusiasm for, because not only didn't he have much interest in the usual pastimes of young men his age, but he rarely showed outward emotion even for things that did excite him. *Feud*, and for some reason Dawson in particular, tickled Luc like nothing else.

Feud binge night happened to coincide with Luc's day off from the March. They passed the morning and early afternoon performing weekly chores. Edna took care of laundry, a task impossible for Luc, what with separating colors from whites and adding the softener mid-cycle. Not to mention ironing, which included sheets and pillowcases, and a folding method for underwear, handed down from her great-great-grandmother. Edna was old-school and believed you could tell a lot about a person by their bureau drawers and linen closets, kitchen cupboards and cleaning-supply shelves, shoe boxes and jewelry caddies. Attention to detail was a trait she held in highest regard. And she'd been pleased when Luc showed an expression of this multi-generational gene, too. Through trial and error, because he wasn't terribly dexterous, she'd winnowed his tasks to vacuuming and feather-dusting. Luc managed all the difficult spots, high and low, with impressive thoroughness and only occasional damage to fragile objects.

"Gram, Gram, Gram! Famous Georges! They got it all!" Luc screamed from the family room.

Edna was still in the kitchen, finishing up hacking away at the onions and garnishing both pizza pies with fresh sprigs of cilantro. She hurried down the hall, plates in each hand, just in time to catch the winning family freak out and Dawson kiss every woman on the lips.

"It was a pretty easy question," she noted. "Remember last week? Name something you do with your nose. Aside from breathing, pretty impossible."

"We know a George. He's kind of famous, isn't he?" Luc asked.

"George Hodges runs the dry cleaner," Edna said, brushing dandruff off Luc's shoulders.

"But he's famous, 'cause everybody's got dry cleaning."

"No one knows him outside Oslo, dear boy. That's not the kind of famous they're talking about."

"Right, Gram," Luc said, regluing himself to Dawson, who'd begun his windup for the next question.

"Name an animal with three letters," Dawson yelled.

"Frog," a woman with crooked teeth answered. Dawson staggered to his knees, laughing.

"That's not right. That's four letters!" Luc scolded the woman badly in need of an orthodontist.

"Where on *earth* do they get these people?" Edna murmured to herself.

"Survey says?!" Dawson screamed at the board, still at the floor weeping.

Beeeeeeeeeeeeep.

They sat side by side in club chairs with TV trays positioned in front. Edna reached over and pinched a few onions she'd missed off Luc's pizza. Maybe she'd call the pizza parlor tomorrow and complain to Leon again. Then she remembered Leon's wife, who gave her a shampoo and set once a week at the Wash and Snip. In the coming months Edna would need Dede's full cooperation, not to mention discretion. No, better to not annoy Leon.

"Do you use narcotics?" Dawson asked the tooth woman, a mother of seven from Lubbock, Texas. Not catching Dawson's nuance, the woman shook her head. Edna wondered how the woman coped with so many children; no wonder she couldn't get her teeth fixed.

Luc turned to Edna with a blank expression. "Gram, what's a narcotic?"

"It's drugs, Luc. The bad ones."

"This lady'll never answer that one right."

"He's asking her because . . . it's not part of the game, dear."

"Oh. Got it, Gram."

Well into the evening, Edna brought in two servings of vanilla ice cream with dollops of Reddi-wip and blue nonpareils sprinkled on top. Even in summer, Maine nights could dip below sixty, and Edna shivered from a sudden deep chill. She excused herself to fetch her treasured ethnic shawl, a gift from one of Edgar's business trips to South America. When she returned not thirty seconds later, Luc had already inhaled his ice cream.

"Couldn't you wait for me?" she asked with a sigh.

"Sorry, Gram," he said, glancing up at her.

"It's okay, dear boy," she whispered, patting his hand.

Luc grabbed her fingers and kissed them one at a time. "Love you, Gram."

She eased back down on her club chair and coiled the shawl around her shoulders and neck.

"Name a famous rabbit," Dawson yelled, his voice straining at high pitch.

"Hippity Hoppity?" a woman with thick glasses guessed tentatively.

"Very clever," Dawson commented. "Survey says?! . . . It's on the board!"

Ding ding ding ding ding.

Edna spooned her dessert, but it didn't seem quite right. Sweet, but definitely a chalky undertone.

"Luc, honey, finish this for me."

"You sure, Gram? Vanilla's your favorite," he said, taking the bowl from her.

"I'm full—too much pizza pie."

Dawson moved to the next family member, a beefy blond with absurd blunt-cut bangs. Well, it was the '80s, Edna reflected.

"Give me the name of a famous rabbit," Dawson repeated.

"Jack Rabbit," the man said with a fist pump.

"My sister used to date him," Dawson disclosed. "Survey says?! . . . Right again!"

Ding ding ding ding ding.

"*Disgusting*," Edna spat.

"Why, Gram?"

"Because Richard Dawson knows no limits. The lewd comments. And all that *kissing*. I've told you that time and again."

"Richard Dawson's smart. He knows all the answers," Luc said.

"He most certainly does *not*," she scolded.

Despite Dawson's preposterous behavior, Edna had to admit that she enjoyed the program and Dawson in particular. He was an outrageous flirt, yes, but intriguing. The bowl haircut. That accent. The whole package held Edna's attention in a way that embarrassed her. Now the family who couldn't come up with "dog" or even "cat" had managed to win the final round, and Edna found this to be poetic justice. Just as she revved up to deliver a lecture to Luc on how folks who got things wrong could still be winners if they just kept on trying, a car crawled up her drive. The headlights blasted through the windows, blinding her.

"See who it is, Luc . . . *Luc!*" she called from the family room, but he was already in the kitchen, washing dishes with the faucet at full throttle. She set aside her TV tray, pushed herself off the chair, and slipped on her shoes, tying the laces in double knots. Before leaving the room, Edna caught a glimpse of her face in the mirror over the fireplace.

The previous day, a neighbor she'd run into at the bakery told her she looked haggard. Edna was so flustered by the rude comment she couldn't summon an appropriate rejoinder. The woman then *hoped nothing was wrong,* and promptly turned away to pinch every last bagel in the basket for freshness. This woman, whose own extended clan was perpetually an anonymous call away from social services, was just one of so many who couldn't help but gossip behind Edna's back. As they'd done when Edgar died and then also poor Sammy. And now with Luc. How disingenuous. To all of Oslo, Edna was *from away* and always would be. They resented her wealth and that she owned prime property on the lake. She was considered a busybody and a know-it-all. Yet they had the gall to ask after her health. How she hated the pretense: thin and obvious. And worse, this woman's comment came on a day she was in terrible pain from the rubber pads chafing her skin where she used to have breasts.

As she lingered by the mirror for a closer look, Edna saw that she did look awful. Her eyebrows were threadbare from the chemo pill, the hair on her head barely holding on. The nurses had advised getting ahead of the hair loss, yet she'd been avoiding any thought of a wig. Maybe now was the time to call that place in Portland and set up an appointment. Edna searched for the pink lipstick she kept in her sweater pocket as she walked to the front door. She dabbed at her lips, then rewrapped Edgar's shawl around her shoulders. My God, she was cold. She posed a smile on her face and opened the door.

"Why, Sandra!" she cried with surprise.

"Sorry to bother you, Edna."

"No bother at *all*. Come on in."

When Pierre poked his head out from behind Sandra, Edna pulled him into her arms and hugged him. He accepted the gesture, shivering in the cool night.

"Where's your jacket? You'll catch your *death*." She removed her shawl and draped it around Pierre's shoulders.

"We hit a deer, Edna. It's dead," Pierre reported with a solemn tone.

"*Lord,* no. That's tragic," Edna said. "Thank goodness you're both okay."

"It's a miracle, but we're fine," Sandra assured her.

"Pierre, darling, Luc's in the kitchen and I'm sure there's enough ice cream left for you. Go on now and let me talk to Sandra."

"Is there chocolate?" Pierre asked.

"You'll take what we have, young man. I know Celine brought you up better than that."

She pushed him toward the kitchen and Pierre skipped down the hallway, her shawl floating behind. Edna ushered Sandra into the formal living room and motioned for them to sit in the overstuffed chairs opposite a teal damask sofa. Sconces with silk shades rimmed the perimeter of the room, and Edna felt certain that in this indirect lighting Sandra wouldn't notice her nonexistent eyebrows and thinning hair.

"He seems *fine*, Sandra," Edna said, now eager to hear about the boy's recent progress in more detail.

"Much more chipper, yes," Sandra concurred.

"And the memory?"

"That was touchy for a bit, but I think I understand what's been happening. His memory is definitely coming back, but he's become quite the little Sartre on the subject,"

"Oh? How so?"

"He's questioning the purpose of memory. He doesn't understand the point of the past or even the future. I wish you'd been there, Edna. Some amazing realizations for a boy his age. But that's our Pierre."

"Yes . . . our Pierre," Edna murmured. "Let me pull the drapes closed," she said suddenly and began to thrust herself off the chair, her arms shaking with effort.

"Easy, Edna. It's a quarter mile up the drive. Nobody can see."

She sank back. "You're right. What's the matter with me? And here it's you who've had the trying night. So. A deer."

"Not exactly. It was that moose who's been roaming," Sandra said, lowering her eyes.

"*No!*" Edna cried.

"I told Pierre it was a deer because I didn't want to upset him. He's seen the animal numerous times. But it was a clean hit, as far as I could tell in the dark," Sandra said, then hesitated. "Edna? Jim and I'll claim the meat."

"Of course. That makes sense. If not you, someone else," she said like a Mainer who knew the score.

Sandra smiled. "Thanks for understanding. We really need it. Anyway, I wanted to call it in to the police tonight, but out of earshot of Pierre. Which is one of the reasons I'm here. Can I use your landline?"

"You know the way." She waved Sandra out of the room.

She listened to Sandra on the phone in the foyer, confirming the accident with the police and committing to the pickup. Edna fully understood the laws and customs around animals killed by cars, and that Sandra and Jim would make full use of the meat. But these days it seemed that all of life was about wreckage. And death. She let her head drop back, hoping the constant pain from the metastases to her spine would let up, even for a moment. Then she heard the boys, now in the family room, trying to imitate Richard Dawson's accent. Edna listened as Pierre brought Luc along in conversation—never superior or tutorial. Such an intuitive soul, he was. She made a mental note to invite him to next week's *Feud* night. Luc was going to need someone like Pierre.

Sandra returned and Edna dragged herself to her feet, rocking back and forth. Sandra held out her hand and Edna grabbed it.

"Careful, Edna. Everything okay?" Sandra asked.

"Of *course*. It's just late and my back acts up at night. What did the cops say?"

"We need to pick it up by seven tomorrow night."

"Did you tell them it was a moose?"

"Had to. We'll have to borrow a truck with a strong winch. If it were a deer there'd be no problem. We've lifted plenty of those with our bare hands."

"I think Luc should drive you two home," Edna said, suddenly wanting to be alone.

"Yeah, I was just going to ask that. I don't trust the car. Lucky it drove even this far."

They were out the door in the next five minutes. Edna returned to the family room and switched off Dawson. She went to the window, looking into pitch black and Maine's thick silence. Even the houses across the lake had gone dark, as if no one lived in them. But Edna could name every single family, their kids' middle names, when they were born, the relations who'd died, what they did for a living, how they spent leisure time, who was ill, and who wasn't happy. Yet these neighbors of many years had shown little curiosity about her, especially after Sammy's death when Edna brought infant Luc home. Those first weeks, walking around the house, hearing nothing but his wail at her shoulder as she jostled him. His cries for food. Perhaps for his mother. Edna doubted anyone in Oslo understood that kind of Maine night. That sort of loneliness.

She sat in the club chair opposite a framed oil painting and shucked off her shoes. The picture was hard to categorize, abstract for sure, yet on close scrutiny the brushstrokes belied a suggestion of three figures clustered together with their arms wrapped around each other. Both the color and mature application still made Edna stop every now and then and examine it closely. Sammy's painting represented a time Edna never wanted to forget.

That final summer, she'd enrolled her daughter in a local art camp. The immersion seemed to provide the stability that Edna had been hoping for. All of Sammy's acting out that had clouded both their lives fell away during those two transformative summer months. Her daughter became more reasonable, helpful. Even kind. More importantly, she'd found joy and purpose in her newfound talent. Then, just before the fall school semester started, Edna had spied Sammy changing clothes in her bedroom. She stood in panties and bra. Her breasts hung heavy, and her belly bloat couldn't be ignored. Sammy stared into the full-length mirror and, seeing Edna in the reflection behind her, made a pretense of sucking in her stomach. She then collapsed into a chair in the corner of the room and cried for a good hour. After some prodding, Sammy confessed she wasn't sure who the father was. This, of course, shocked Edna, but only for a moment. They were Sibleys—proud and protective of their own. She promised Sammy they'd face Oslo together and make a life with her child. The picture in the den had been Sammy's final painting, and those next months, waiting for Luc's birth, were the best of their lives.

On any other night, she would have waited for Luc to return and they'd lock up the house together, one of many things Edna was teaching him these days. For the future. Instead, she climbed the stairs and swallowed her chemo pill along with a sedative, which she took only on nights like this. When hounding from her past and worries for Luc's future kept her on edge. Which then made her think of Pierre and his existential awakening. In this way Pierre was very much like Sammy in those last months before her death, as Edna now recalled how her daughter had lived every day in the moment.

Edna crawled between the linen sheets with her clothes still on. She undid the clasp to her pearls and dropped them onto the nightstand. The sound was thick, like spongy stones. She tugged on her wedding rings, easing them over the wrinkles at her knuckle, and clustered them next to the pearls. Lying on her side, Edna stared at the treasures from her marriage. A Chinois enameled pill caddy lay hidden under Edgar's pillow. She slipped her hand in and touched it, surprised at how warm the thing was. Edgar's wedding ring slipped out. Smothering the ring in her fist, Edna drew it close to her chest scars and rolled onto her back. She bore the pain in her spine. "Not yet, darling. But soon."

BATHING IS NOT OVERRATED

SINCE THEIR HEATING SYSTEM HAD GONE down the drain Sandra had, indeed, been reduced to bathing every third day. In between, she sufficed with a chilly wipe-down at the sink. Jim, on the other hand, tried to hold on to the belief that beginning each morning with a stone-cold shower was not only invigorating but might even improve brain function. That optimistic theory collapsed before the first week was out. He still took a shower daily but now doused himself in less than sixty seconds, cursing all the way.

With the house steeped in seven a.m. quiet, day number three had finally arrived and Sandra was more than eager for a full-immersion soak. Four teakettles sat on four burners in the kitchen, their whistles screaming within seconds of each other. She toted them upstairs two by two and set them on the slate floor beside the already-filled claw-foot tub. Infusing hot water a little at a time, Sandra swished with her hand until the temperature felt optimal. She then lowered herself in and stretched out her legs, once again grateful for having scavenged this long soaker from the town dump years earlier. Tension from her accident with the moose the previous night finally eased. After a while, when the water began to cool, she reached for the third kettle. Warmth sluiced over her head and shoulders. She then got busy and sponged her underarms, cleaned between toes, and pumiced calloused heels. She rubbed and rinsed, again and again. And it all felt like the eighth wonder of the world.

While reveling in her ablutions, Sandra also tinkered with the notion of optimism. A good-sized windfall had been set in motion by the crash. And while Sandra never dreamed that she'd be one of those Mainers who viewed roadkill as a means by which she'd stock her freezer, she was also acquainted with the unspoken gospel according to Oslo. Which went something like, when somebody rammed their car into an animal, that unfortunate death would drastically improve somebody's dinner. Yet, *that* moose. Sandra took a deep breath, dunked her head underwater, and deliberated. Maybe she'd call the cops and tell them to go ahead and release the moose to someone else. She thought she remembered that in cases of unclaimed roadkill, the meat, if collected soon enough, went to charity. No, that was just plain foolish. The animal was *food*. By the time she surfaced to take a breath, Sandra concluded she might as well join the club and dine on the moose for as long as possible. Anyway, if she and Jim weren't Mainers by now, she didn't know what they were.

A knuckle rapped at the door. Jim poked his head in. "Can I come in?"

"Don't let the steam escape," she said, waving him into the bathroom.

Jim closed the door, wiped the mirror over the sink of fog, and brushed his teeth.

"I just called . . . reserved the truck . . . they'll take some meat . . . as payment . . . ," he said between brushing, rinsing, and spitting.

"Sounds like a plan. Now make yourself really useful and wash my hair."

Jim propped himself on the edge of the tub and dug a small wad of Sandra's soft homemade soap from a glass mason jar.

"You'll need more than that—it's been three days," she reminded him with a thin smile.

"Yes, boss," he said, and clawed another clump.

Jim pushed Sandra's torso forward. He gathered up the length of her hair to the crown of her head, then mashed in the soap, creating a concoction that looked like loose oatmeal. With the flats of his fingers, he massaged her scalp. Sandra released a low moan. Hidden muscles still ached in odd places. She arched her back, then re-collapsed, hanging her head between her knees.

"Am*aaa*zing," she whispered into the water. "I think I love you."

"Well, thank fuck for *that*."

She looked up at him, wiping a clump of soap from her forehead. "Get in the tub."

"Do we have time?"

"The moose isn't going anywhere."

"It's awkward . . . my back."

"*Try*. Jesus."

Jim kicked his boxers to the side, stepped in, and sat opposite. Sandra slid underwater to rinse her hair. Then she sacrificed the final kettle, pouring hot water over Jim's head. Steam rose up and they remained this way for a few minutes, watching the water, dense with soap, eddy around their limbs.

"Let's plan the day," Jim suggested.

"Not yet. This is too much heaven," Sandra said, rolling her head from side to side on the back rim of the tub. "See what you've been missing? All those idiotic showers."

"True," he conceded. "Why don't I listen to you more often?"

"No idea."

He used his feet to pry her legs open and she let her knees fall to either side of the tub. Jim placed the ball of his foot on Sandra's pussy. She adjusted so that her clitoris was in direct contact, then edged forward to create more pressure.

"Right. There," she encouraged.

Jim brought her to a quick orgasm.

"I do love you," she managed between pants, eyes shut tight.

"You said that already." He laughed.

"When I'm sex-ditsy I repeat myself."

"You're beautiful when you aren't thinking."

"Which is practically never, right?" Sandra said, spying at him with one eye open.

"I didn't mean it that way," Jim said defensively.

She stretched her legs out and as Jim moved over to make room, she noticed his penis was hard.

"Can we?" she asked.

"On the bed."

"Your back is better?"

He didn't answer. Instead, Jim stood and reached for her hands in order to pull her up. They stepped out of the tub and he used a large bath towel to dry them both off, then wrapped her dripping hair into a terry-cloth turban. When he nestled her from behind, his hands cupping her breasts, she felt his erection pressing against her butt. This was Jim: his kind attention and an eager body. And somehow this goodness managed to counterbalance Sandra's tendency to assume less-than-optimal conclusions about most things and then think an additional five steps ahead with dread. A man with a greater career drive and who provided more financial stability would certainly have mitigated those habits. But she welcomed, and was grateful for, Jim's easy stare across the kitchen table every morning. Because though they still occasionally broke each other's hearts in ways they didn't bother to discuss anymore, in the end, Jim's failings were nothing earth-shattering. Not even original. Forgivable.

Sandra was aching for the sex by now, and Jim certainly knew this. But he held off, rubbing her hair dry, working from scalp to split ends. Then he fluffed the strands out, plucking with his fingers the way he'd learned from watching her try to create some volume from pin-straight hair. Finally, Jim kissed the back of her neck and led her into the bedroom. He sat in a chair and Sandra kneaded his shoulders, gently broaching his lower back. They always attended to each other this way—a mutual forestalling. And Sandra was particularly thankful for the delay now, because she detected unfamiliar perfume on his Grateful Dead T-shirt she'd just scooped off the floor.

She turned to look out the window. The sky was azure blue, portending a pleasant day to pick up the moose. A raven landed on top of Jim's greenhouse roof and she remembered that the latest crop of lettuce was due to be harvested for that night's dinner. Within those few seconds, while pondering other forces of nature, Sandra found her way back from the dark side of her imagination. Because Jim's attention and affection toward her had never, ever waned. Not even once.

She turned back to find him watching her, now from the bed. Allowing the Grateful Dead to drop from her hand, Sandra saw Jim track the shirt until it hit the floor. He closed his eyes for about five seconds, then refocused at her face but didn't smile. Sandra cat-walked across the mattress and flopped onto her back. Jim ran his hand across her breasts, rubbing her nipples, then pumped himself to get hard again. She felt for his cock with one hand while fingering herself with the other. Sandra was wet, and smiled at him to signal that she was ready. But instead of entering her, Jim crumpled his body into a ball and cupped both hands around her ear as if what he was about to whisper might change the course of their lives. And yes, his next words shook her. How he needed her more than he wanted her. How he'd want her forever. And that he loved her in a way he'd never imagined possible. Neither moved for several seconds, which seemed like minutes and which, to Sandra, felt like a miracle.

"Don't leave me," he said, grabbing her hand without looking at her face.

"You don't know by now?" she asked.

"I need to hear it."

"I'll never leave you, Jim."

"Again. *Please.*"

"There isn't anything you could do that would make me go. Nothing." She'd never meant it more.

"I'm so tired. I don't know why."

She tangled her arms and legs around him and squeezed tight, as much as her muscles could give. He gasped from her power. They fell asleep, entwined like Pompeiian figures in mid-motion, but woke at intervals to see if the other was still there. The morning evaporated.

Later, at midday, while they ate sandwiches and drank sour lemonade, Sandra and Jim plotted out the next couple of hours with the precision of air-traffic controllers. They'd gutted and sectioned animals on occasion and with some competency, but never anything as large as a moose. And because she still felt ambivalence about this particular animal, Sandra very much wanted to depersonalize the slaughter. So, taking all this into consideration, they called an experienced butcher several towns over who agreed to not only prepare the moose, but also take meat as payment.

The truck had been delivered while they'd slept and now sat parked outside, next to her motorbike. While Jim got acquainted with various gears and tested the winch and ropes, Sandra cleaned up the lunch dishes and made confirmation calls to those children she'd teach the next day. Oddly, it was the parents who tended to forget their own kid's lesson; she'd been burned more than a few times, making the drive only to find the student wasn't even home. So, she'd recently begun checking in the day before—annoying and time-consuming, yet necessary. She'd just finished with the last student's father, who had no clue about the lesson but promised his kid would be there, when Edna phoned to apologize for her behavior the previous evening, something Sandra noticed was becoming a habit with her.

"Thanks for lending us Luc for the drive home," Sandra said. "We'll come get the car tomorrow if that's okay with you. But Edna, forgive me. I need to ask again. What's going on with you?"

"Nothing. *Really*. I've been tired is all. Though right now I'm terribly worried because Luc didn't come home last night."

"Oh? Maybe he went to the Robinet and stayed late. Slept in his truck? You've mentioned he's done that before. Come to think of it, I did notice he didn't turn back toward your house after he dropped me off."

"I'm trying to let him be, give him independence. But . . . I suppose I'll wait till evening before calling the police."

"The *police*? No. You're completely overthinking this. Look, Jim and I are off to pick up the moose right now. We should be home in a couple hours. I'll check back with you then. But don't call the police, Edna. You don't want them in your business. Anyway, I'm sure he'll show up any minute."

"You're right. Fine . . ." Edna trailed off.

"Wait for my call. Okay?"

"Yes, yes. Good, Sandra, I feel better."

Jim honked and she grabbed one of his caps off a coat peg, stuffed her hair into it, and hurried to the truck. In spite of the warm weather, they'd donned heavy work jeans, long-sleeved shirts, and waterproof boots, all as protection from the potentially filthy work. Jim reached over, took her hand, and pulled her into the cab. He grinned, his face full of excitement, and she was happy to take his cue. Sandra patted Jim's knee. "Come on, big boy. Let's go pick up dinner."

As they drove, and now in daylight, Sandra found it baffling that she couldn't locate where the accident had occurred. Admittedly, she and Pierre hadn't paid any attention to their surroundings, particularly during their intense exchange while on the interstate. And once they'd hit the county road, with nothing but pitch black outside and singing to music at full volume inside, the time had passed as if suspended. Until they hit the moose. Still, Sandra was more than frustrated after they'd traveled the entire distance from the fork on the lake road to the ramp leading onto the interstate. Jim turned the truck around and parked on the side of the road. They sat in silence, listening to the engine groan.

"This is weird," Sandra finally declared.

"Think. What do you remember? Details."

She unbuckled her seat belt and propped her feet onto the dashboard. Jim opened a thermos of coffee and offered her a swig. She imagined the caffeine sweeping a mental fog aside, because when she thought about the previous night, it did feel more like a dream than reality.

"Okay. She fell into the woods down a shallow embankment. I'm guessing thirty feet or so off the road. A patch of low trees was broken at the roadside. That's how I first spotted her, because the car happened to be angled in that direction and the headlights were on. I went a few feet past the trees, and that's when I saw her rear end. But Jim, the back windshield was shattered. Wouldn't we have seen glass on the road, or at least felt it under the tires?"

Jim rubbed his unshaven chin, thinking. "Maybe. But it might have blown mostly into the car rather than out. The slant. Make sense?"

"Right, and Pierre commented that the pellets were beautiful. He'd scooped them up from the backseat. So, yes. But the car swiveled a lot. I remember trying to correct with steering. Braking made things worse, of course. You'd think we'd have seen some evidence of skid marks."

"Not necessarily. Our tires are pretty bald, and worn rubber tends to glide rather than grab the pavement," Jim said.

"Yeah, it did feel like I was on ice. Too smooth."

"God. Tires. Another thing to replace. Maybe we should just junk the car," Jim suggested.

"What? No way. That monster saved our lives last night."

"Funny. *I'm* the one who usually wants to hang on to useless stuff," Jim said, laughing.

"Role reversal. A sure sign of a successful marriage," she said.

"We'll keep the car," he said, stroking her cheek. "Just don't ask me to start teaching cello."

"Slim chance of that. C'mon. Let's head back and this time drive really, really slowly."

The truck was, it turned out, quite a wreck, and even more dicey at the slower speed. Its shocks weren't up to absorbing the seemingly endless potholes dotting the county road. Threadbare seats didn't help matters either. Sandra, with no ass to speak of, grabbed a blanket from the back and placed it on her seat to help absorb the assault to her sitz bones. And it felt a strain all the more because the accident continued to show up in seldom-used muscles all over her body. Meanwhile, Jim knuckled the steering wheel, toggling from first gear to second and back per Sandra's instructions as she scrutinized the road.

"There it is!" Sandra finally yelled, grabbing Jim's shoulder.

"Thank God," Jim said, and rolled to a stop.

"Back up about twenty feet," she said.

He shifted, and the truck stuttered in reverse until Sandra gave the signal. She jumped out, leaving the door ajar, and stood at the precipice to the shallow slope.

"She's gone!" Sandra cried, pointing.

Jim ran around the truck and joined her. "Get back in the truck, Sandra. *Now*."

"Why?"

"Something's not right here."

"But I want to—Oh my God. Jim . . . *no*."

There was nothing more either could say or do but succumb to what lay in front of them. As they walked down the slope hand in hand, their boots sank slightly into moist soil. Which seemed wrong, because Oslo had experienced something of a drought over the past weeks. Then the sun broke through to expose an unexpected color spewed across the needled ground cover. Deep red. Undeniably moose blood. Sandra crouched down and placed her glove on the color, which was at turns damp and dry. She looked up at Jim.

"Who would do this?" she said, almost crying as she wiped the blood on some leaves.

Jim only shook his head. They continued to turn around and around, bewildered and shocked by the destruction before them. Nearby lay odd body parts. Hoofs, hacked about a foot up on each leg, stacked like pipes against a tree. Two ears with a tail in between, arranged in a neat row. And at random, the dewlap, and what looked like the heart and other unidentifiable organs. This was a brutal butchering, but organized, slightly ritualistic. And, somehow worse, with no regard for any sane hunter's ethical transaction with nature.

"This is a *crime*," Sandra said with quiet rage.

"Yes, it is. But have you noticed what's not here? The actual body. And the *head*," Jim said.

Her stomach roiled. Sandra began to collapse but Jim caught her by the arm, preventing her from falling on the gore all around their feet. As they held each other, she closed her eyes, not wanting to look. How had she missed registering what was missing? Then again, to look into the animal's eyes would have forced her to acknowledge that, yes, this is what people do. The moose's only consistent and unchecked danger, other than a pack of wolves, was a human toting a gun or driving a car.

Sandra couldn't begin to unravel her feelings of sadness, confusion, anger. And complicity.

Back in the truck, having wiped their boots of blood, they took a few minutes to calm down. Sandra pulled a plastic container of water up from the floorboard and they took turns drinking, trying to organize their emotions into some sort of reasonable plan of action.

"The thing is, no one could have seen the moose just by driving by," Jim said finally. "Someone had to know."

"The cops. Edna. That's all," she said.

"Pierre?"

"I told him it was a deer."

"What about Luc?"

Sandra sighed. "It's possible Pierre told him when Edna and I were talking in the living room."

"That's it, then. I never bought that Forrest Gump act. Even if he thought he was picking up a deer, that guy not only committed a crime, he's a fucking sadist."

"You don't know that, Jim. It's completely out of character for Luc. He's really quite passive. I'd rather think it was the cops. Remember when Lucinda and Bob hit a big buck a couple years ago?"

"Yeah?"

"Well, they called it in, and it went missing too. Turns out the person at the police station who took their call told a relative a couple of towns over. Bob made a huge fuss. They finally told him who stole it. When he picked it up a few hours later the thing had already been skinned and completely butchered. Bob said it was really creepy."

"Who was on the phone last night at the station?"

"Andrea."

"She doesn't seem the type," Jim said. "A straight arrow. Kind of prissy."

"I've heard she's a weird control freak who tells her husband when to piss," Sandra said. "In any case, let's take it slow. I don't want to go anywhere near Luc as a possibility before we know more. And Edna's been so off lately. I don't think she could take it, Jim. Anyway, does it really matter? Whoever took it, that scene down there pretty much guarantees that we've already lost the meat."

"True enough," Jim agreed.

Sitting in the truck and from the higher vantage point, Sandra looked down the slope and was able to make out the gruesome remains of someone's idea of theft. She held on to the belief that Luc had not done this; he'd only ever presented as benign and gentle, which made the very thought unfathomable. But over the years there'd been so many odd events in Oslo that at first seemed impossible and then got folded into quaint town folklore. Now, she simply wanted to assume the cops were to blame and forget the whole episode. But Sandra knew better—some sort of disappointment was surely to come.

THE SUM OF ONE ANIMAL

MUCH OF THE PROFIT FOR THE ROBINET coincided with shift changes at the March. Having just completed his, Claude had sequestered himself in a corner booth. Across the dimly lit room, a frantic solo bartender threw drinks down for three-deep bar patrons. Most heated a bar stool with devotion and knocked back shots with beer chasers, trying to come down from the stress of factory work. Hopefuls scanned for hookups, while a few couples tried the dance floor. Claude's foot jittered to the confusing jukebox selection, a song with no melody by some rapper with one letter and four numbers for a name. He could have done with a few belts of whiskey to render the atmosphere more appealing. But Claude meant to stay sober. He nursed his third ginger ale, running numbers on the recent monies brought in through his soon-to-be-shuttered meat business.

It was mildly risky, exposing his ledger and calculator to the three a.m. crowd. But because Claude was famous for being less than civil at the end of a double shift, he could pretty well count on a wide berth. In truth, his current mood had nothing to do with having clocked twelve hours. Or the fact that his son had been abducted by Saint Sandra to attend one of her flimflam concerts in Portland. Or that Celine hadn't answered when he'd called earlier that evening and if she was out, where in hell had she gone to? No, none of that. It was all about the damned numbers, and they weren't behaving.

After adding the column three times, two totals had jibed, which normally would have satisfied him as accurate. But the third was considerably higher. So he decided to run it once more to see if a fourth calculation would match the greater sum. If this worked out, and he *almost* hoped it would, Claude meant to earmark the money for a new violin for Pierre. The Saint, through Celine as proxy, had been hinting for weeks. He placed a bar napkin over the "total" screen so he couldn't see the numbers as they increased, and then slowly punched in each number with what he imagined was *real* accuracy. *Merde.* Not only had the calculator produced an altogether different total, but it was *lower* than the previous three. Disgusted, Claude propped his elbows on the table and buried his face in his hands. He wasn't good at math. That was Celine's thing; she could add endless columns in her head, even on pills.

Claude blindly swatted the calculator to the side. At the same time, someone clomped up and stopped at his table. The so-and-so seemed to be breathing through its mouth and nose simultaneously, if that was even possible. Lordy. He was in his booth not bothering a living soul, smoking like a lifer and unhappily sober. *Obviously* not open for pleasure or business. He gave the snuffer five more seconds to back off and when he/she/it didn't get the message, Claude looked up to see something he really didn't need right now. Luc Sibley. Claude snapped the ledger shut with a bang, which blew his pencil off the table.

"I thought this was *Feud* night," Claude said with a sigh, scraping the pencil off the floor.

"It is."

"What're you doing here?" he asked.

"*Feud* ends at ten."

"How's your boyfriend, Dawson?"

"Really good. But I don't think Gram likes him."

"Well, she's a bright lady. *She* knows. He's a Brit. A snob."

"Snob? Like how?"

"A know-it-all. Like Saint Kimbrough."

"Oh. Can I have a Cherry Coke?"

"You're over twenty-one, for *merde* sake. Get it yourself!" Claude barked.

"I'm twenty-nine," Luc corrected.

"I *know* how old you are. It's an expression."

Luc snuffed—out, in, out.

"Oh, forget it," Claude said, shooing him away. Luc waded through bodies for a minute or two and returned with his Coke. Three maraschino cherries floated on top of ice cubes.

"Mrs. Kimbrough says I shouldn't eat the cherries," Luc announced, sliding into the corner much too close to Claude.

"This isn't a sleepover. Move *over*," Claude said, shoving him a few feet away.

"She says they stay at the bottom of your stomach for a week," Luc continued.

"You gonna listen to *her*? She's got more rules to live by than Moses on the mount. Anyway, I happen to know that's a lie."

"Mrs. Kimbrough lies?"

"'Course she does. Go ahead and eat your dinner." Claude winked, pointing at the cherries.

Luc tongued all three cherries into his mouth, ripping the stems off with his front teeth. He chewed about four times then washed the clump down with one giant swallow. Claude swept the stems from the tabletop onto the floor with his forearm. He stared at the calculator and considered a fifth and absolute final stab, while Luc fingernailed red flecks out of his back molars.

"Listen to me. Kimbrough? You can't trust her. *Or* him," Claude warned. "Just remember that."

"What about Gram?" Luc asked tentatively.

"Your gram's a good woman. She asked me to be your friend, didn't she? How's that turned out?"

"Pretty good, I guess."

While Luc gawked at a flock of females herding by the bar, Claude went back to imagining collateral fallout from his calculator drama. If he did add the column a fifth time and it actually matched the higher number, then he'd be forced to consult with the Saint. She'd advise him on what instrument to buy and he'd have no choice but to take her word for it, because she was the expert. And Claude hated the thought that the Saint just might be an expert at anything, other than as a leech lording over his son. Pierre was brilliant, the Saint declared. Her most talented student ever, she claimed. No limit to how far he could go, she predicted. A career in music was a given, she insisted. Nope. Nope. Nope. And *nope*. He'd go with the original total. Be done with the new violin idea. Break the news to Celine. Maybe make up for it with that pair of Jimmy Choos she'd been whining about. And merciful Jesus, that so-called song had finally finished.

Claude stubbed out his third-to-last cigarette. "So. What's this meeting about?" he asked Luc.

"Deer."

"What about 'em?"

"One got killed."

"How? The trap?"

"A car. I found it on the road."

"Yeah?"

"Uh-huh."

"Okay, let's go get it!"

"I did it."

"*You* hit the deer?" Claude asked, skeptical.

"I got the deer."

"*You got the deer*," Claude said, exasperated that he was parroting Luc's words.

"Uh-huh."

"What the fuck do you *mean*? Where is it?"

"At the meat shed. I picked it up after *Feud*. That's why I'm here." Luc managed a smidgen of a smile.

"Mother of *Dieu*. Why didn't you tell me this twelve and a half minutes ago?"

They took Luc's truck. Claude insisted on driving, because Luc strictly obeyed red lights per Edna, and at this late hour Claude didn't have patience for any color. He floored the gas pedal, thinking green all the way. They reached the other side of the Hump in record time, then headed around the perimeter of the March and parked near the meat shed.

Windows punctured three sides of the building, and lights shining from the inside pooled everywhere, broadcasting that the abandoned structure had been in use. Claude watched Luc kneel down to retie his bootlaces, naïve to how he'd just jeopardized the operation. He should have gone crazy on him, as this was a major breach of protocol. Instead, he felt himself ease into uncharacteristic forgiveness. After all, the windows were just under the roofline and too high for anyone to see inside without a ladder, so no real harm was done. As they walked closer, he saw that Luc had remembered to padlock the metal door, which was much more important than the lights. And yes, he was pleased with Luc's first-ever contribution to the business—not some squirrel or chipmunk as he'd expect from the man, but an actual dead deer. And already delivered for butchering, no less. It showed initiative, which was exactly what he'd been asked by Edna to teach him. He patted Luc's back, encouraging him to unlock the door, and like buddies in crime they stepped into the meat shed.

Once inside, Luc immediately backed away from Claude. He leaned against a cement wall and slid to the floor—a strange habit Claude had witnessed more than a few times. Edna explained it away, calling the motion a "preemptive concession to defeat." To Claude, this was pure psychobabble and just another example of a spoiled brat's manipulation. He believed that Luc could be brought around like a dog via the tried-and-true treat/punishment method. But the problem with any dog was, there was always that one time when the urge to go after a squirrel outweighed the command of the master. Luc was now rocking back and forth with his arms wrapped around his knees, whining a sustained whimper like a puppy locked in a crate.

"Quiet," Claude commanded. The noise stopped.

The first thing that hit Claude was the odor: meat on the edge and in need of immediate icing or it would succumb to rot. Then he noticed blood splattered everywhere on the cement—still wet and puddling into dips in the floor. On the butchering platform the animal's back was to him, but nothing about this deer made any sense. He began a slow walk to the right of the animal and saw that the tail had been severed, its rectum visible, which caused the thing to present as vulnerable. Claude briefly averted his eyes with bashfulness. Then the legs, unnaturally short, without hoofs. Sinew and tendons and bones had been hacked in a sloppy and cruel way, and Claude couldn't help but cover his mouth. As he moved to the front of the animal, he saw the belly had been slashed open, stem to stern, and the organs gutted out. Ribs could not adequately prevent the flank from caving, so there was an unnatural hollow to its midsection.

The torso itself had been cut into large sections and then reassembled on the platform. An earless head looked to be tagged on at the end, almost as an afterthought—like some crazy mortician's joke.

Then all the horror seemed to come together in one single feature. The nose. Claude staggered backward. This was a *moose*. He re-examined the midsection. Scars. *Mon Dieu. That* moose.

Luc lifted his head and began to stutter an explanation. "Claude . . . see . . . I . . ."

"Shut the fuck up."

"But—"

In three giant steps, Claude was there. He grabbed Luc under the armpits and pulled him up from the floor, pinning his back to the wall. "If there was ever a time in your sorry, useless life you needed to follow my instructions, it's now. Shut. *Up*." He let go and backed up several paces. Luc folded back down and covered his head with his arms.

"Where did this thing come from?" Claude asked, trying to control himself.

"Pierre."

Claude felt his leg haul back and watched his boot land hard, directly into Luc's midsection. The sheer force of the torque pushed Claude off the floor several inches, a sensation that gratified, because for one split second he was flying and free from the rage that tore through his body.

"Don't make me drag it out of you. Where'd you get this animal?"

"*Pierre*," Luc whispered, aiming the name into his knees, which he'd now clamped to his chest.

"That's not possible," Claude said, but knew it was probably true. If nothing else, Luc was incapable of lying.

"I swear it. He said they hit a deer—"

"It's a goddamned *moose*! Can't you even see that? Wait. Was Pierre with *Celine*?" The Frankenstein moose now bled away, the least of his problems. His family had been in an accident. They were frightened. Maybe hurt. And though he hadn't been with them, the sense of his own culpability felt real and intolerable.

"No. Mrs. Kimbrough," Luc said, rubbing his eyes.

Somehow, Claude didn't feel relieved in the least. The woman who'd brainwashed his son in broad daylight using that stinking violin as her tool was, it seemed, driving Pierre all over creation in the dead of night, getting into accidents and killing animals along the way. Claude wondered, for what seemed like the millionth time, *how on God's green earth* she'd gotten control over his family.

"Tell me Pierre's okay."

"He's okay."

Claude sat on the floor next to Luc and pulled the man's cap off, lobbing it over the moose. It landed on the other side of the shed in a pool of blood. "You're gonna tell me exactly what happened if we have to sit here till the last priest is arrested for buggering boys."

Luc looked in the opposite direction.

"C'mon. Get on with it."

"Mrs. Kimbrough and Pierre came over tonight."

"*Why* is this woman messing with my family?" Claude bellowed rhetorically at the ceiling.

"I was in the kitchen with Pierre, eating ice cream. That's when he told me they hit a deer on the county road. That's when Gram told me to drive them home 'cause the car got banged up in the crash. That's when I decided to look for the deer."

"Christ on a swing."

"I wanted to show you. I can get meat, *too*."

"Cut the Fredo act. How in hell did you get an entire moose here?" he asked.

"It was gonna get cut up anyway, so I did it there."

"Oh, please no. On the *road*?"

"It was more in the woods. I had tools in the truck."

"Did anybody see you?"

"I worked quick."

"Obviously," Claude said, briefly glancing at the hatchet job. "Okay, Luc. I'm going to get you out of this mess."

Within an hour they had the moose chopped up and thrown, piece by piece, into the incinerator. Claude hosed down the shed, making sure every last splatter of blood was rinsed completely from the floor and walls. The place hadn't been this clean since the business began. When dawn broke, they pulled everything out of Luc's truck and doused it with water and antiseptic cleaner. After they changed their clothes into spare shirts and jeans stored at the shed, Claude reminded Luc about turning off the lights, pointing out that he'd made a mistake. With schooled deliberation, Luc pushed down on the bank of switches and they walked out the door.

"How're you feeling?" Claude asked amiably as he locked up the shed.

"Okay."

Claude patted Luc's midsection and tousled his hair. "Sorry about that."

Luc nodded, then looked away.

"How's about we sit on the bench here and rest up awhile? Then we'll get some breakfast."

As they sat, Claude flexed his hands and arms, which ached from the hard labor. He looked at his blood-spattered boots. He'd have to throw them out when he returned home, a pity to be sure. But a beauty of a morning was beginning in Oslo—that sweetness of a cloudless sky, the air still cool. The din of the March pulsed in the background and he was grateful to have a job that he could count on. These were the things that made sense, and Claude now felt content, even optimistic. He glanced at his watch—just after seven. His stomach growled in the best way and he found himself looking forward to a filling meal of eggs, potatoes, juice, maybe a donut too. No coffee, but a beer to take off the edge. Then home for some solid, well-deserved sleep. Because his family was safe.

"You can't talk about this. The moose and all. Right?" Claude said, poking Luc in the arm.

"Yeah," Luc said.

"You sure? This is important."

"Uh-huh."

"It's got to be like it never happened. 'Cause if anybody ever found out that you butchered that moose, especially the *way* you did it? I don't even want to think what that would do to your gram."

"I know—"

"Do ya?" Claude broke in. "It'd break her in two."

Luc nodded.

"And my son," Claude continued. "He knew that moose. Now he's going to wonder what happened to her and I'm going to have to feed him some bullshit story about the ways of nature. And Pierre's no fool."

"I get it."

"I hope so. Because the other thing is, you stole that moose from Mrs. Kimbrough. It was her crash, so the meat's supposed to be hers. You took it and that's a crime."

"A crime . . ."

"No. I need you to understand. When I say it's a *crime*, I mean you could get in trouble with the cops—"

"Can we get breakfast at the IHOP?" Luc interrupted with a massive yawn. His head dropped to the side and landed against Claude's shoulder. The snuffing regulated down to shallow breathing and just like that, the man fell asleep.

From a distance, the scene might have looked like they were friends who shared a long history that made such proximity reasonable. But for Claude, contact between men was uncomfortable because he couldn't trust where it came from. Like fancy food—manipulated beyond its natural state. It certainly wasn't natural that Luc could fall asleep like a baby after having just decapitated a moose. And it wasn't natural, or even fair, that Claude himself had labored like a farm animal to yet again clean up this fool's trail of mindless destruction. No. On this perfect Maine morning, nothing on the Lord's planet was in any way natural. Because, Luc. Who'd brought Pierre to the shed, which led to his memory loss. Luc, who then defied Claude by not burying that moose calf. Luc, who finally did manage to pick up an animal on his own—but the exact *wrong* animal. Luc, who was trying to play at life like a man but would forever be a child. And Luc, who now wanted his breakfast at the IHOP?

Luc never saw it coming. The left jab that smashed his orbital bone. The right hook that caught his jaw and propelled him a foot in the air. The hard kick to his groin. The one, two cheap shots to his kidneys. The pummeling, pummeling, pummeling at his midsection. Claude, staring at Luc flat on his back, his limbs pinwheeled to the ground, not moving. Claude, panting like a bull, not caring if Luc ever took another breath. Claude, walking away.

GOD GRANT ME THE SERENITY

TWO CHAIRS AND A ROLLING TABLE littered with canisters filled with cotton balls, tongue depressors, and nasal swabs took up all but a few square feet of the claustrophobic examination room. When Claude dropped into a chair on one side of the table, he immediately felt uncomfortably moist. It reminded him of his office at the March: virtually zero ventilation and a portending of no way out. Sweat tunneled down his face, his breath shallowed up. He rubbed clammy palms back and forth on his thighs.

"Do you know your blood type, Mr. Roy?" the technician asked as he labeled multiple glass tubes.

"Isn't that what you're here for?" he answered with a smirk. Claude had no clue about his blood; he'd never been curious about such things.

"Just making conversation," the man placated.

"Just get on with it," Claude said, rolling up his sleeve.

He wrapped a tourniquet around Claude's bicep and flicked two fingers at the crook of his elbow, like in some movie about heroin addicts. Claude had always wondered if they really needed to do that. As the needle disappeared into his vein, he averted his eyes, landing on a poster listing the Twelve Steps with the Serenity Prayer tagged at the end. His bowels moved an inch. When the guy asked him to squeeze his fist, no doubt another cliché, Claude winced. That the swelling and bruising on his knuckles had lasted this long surprised him, because Luc had submitted to the beating like an agreeable punching bag. In fact, he couldn't recall any particular blow severe enough to have made his hand ache this badly, let alone cause Luc's coma. Going on a week, now.

Much of that night had gone missing. Similar to when, every now and again, he'd allow himself a major drunk and wake up not remembering (or caring, for that matter) who he'd pissed off. Now, sitting in the chair, trying very hard to not stare at the chronic acne on the technician's face, Claude was only able to claw back sensory memories. Such as sound. Screaming, surely his own. Fist on flesh. Crying, which he assumed came from Luc, but it seemed plausible he'd joined in at some point. Then color. Red spread across grey. Dirt-brown fur. The bluest sky, just before something about the IHOP. But what Claude *could* conjure up with too much clarity was the condition of the moose. Holes. Shredded bones. Floppy tendons. A missing dewlap. Its nose. And those scars. All week long, he'd fallen asleep to these particular indignities floating behind eyes slammed shut. Even dreamt about them as assaults to his own body. Then he'd wake and for about an hour feel ambivalence about the hurt he'd caused Luc. But coma be damned, Claude simply couldn't forgive Luc's butchering work, the likes of which no Mainer with a quarter brain and a sliver of a heart would ever stand for. He closed his eyes and felt the needle nudge around in his vein as the technician switched out the tubes.

"Almost done. Only the donation bag now," the man said.

Claude grunted. As if this were some comfort. Leave it to Luc to be even more "special," as Edna recently christened him, with a weird blood type. Then of course, the Saint couldn't help herself from butting in. She rallied the entire town around this bloodletting nonsense, hyping it into an all-out campaign to root out an equally special donor, and while they were at it replenish the blood banks. Claude viewed the pressure as a cheap threat. Like, either run five miles for the cure for cancer or forever be seen as a layabout. Besides, everyone in Oslo knew if you got any sort of cancer, what with local pollution, you were pretty much a goner. Now all the jabber at the Robinet, the hardware store, Shaw's, and even at the March, was how every last cousin twice removed had opened their veins. Just the other day, Claude had been cornered at the car wash by no less than three people who, when he'd admitted he'd not yet donated, called him heartless, *selfish*. A man could barely tend to his daily chores without being reminded of Luc's blood and his coma.

"There you go, Mr. Roy," the man said, ripping off the rubber strap. "Better grab a glass of orange juice. You might feel woozy for a while."

Claude rolled his eyes and headed directly for the john. The three urinals were already in use; it seemed everyone was pissing Tropicana. He stepped into a stall, pushed his jeans down to his boots and landed hard on the toilet seat. Damn. He did feel dizzy, and now regretted ignoring the nurse with the nice set of boobs when she tried to shove a plastic cup into his hand. As he'd walked past her, she winked at him, and now Claude remembered that she was the bartender that night with Luc at the Robinet. Did she know?

During the past week, Claude had retraced his steps by spritzing the shed again and then personally dismantled all the traps. He even burned the ledger and crushed the calculator with the heel of his boot. A few days later, he made like a real executive and took apart his makeshift office. This meant the business was officially dead, the moose up in ashes. And the wink was surely nothing more than harmless flirting.

But dear God. Now he couldn't feel his feet. Claude dropped his head between his knees. The black and white penny tiles on the floor seemed to wave at him. Dragging his arms up, he managed to place his hands on the stall door to keep himself from falling forward and passing out. And he couldn't understand why he felt so shitty because things were, at least at home, looking up.

Celine had pulled herself off the pills. The day after the Luc thing, and while Claude slept well into the afternoon, apparently Celine had a heart-to-heart with herself. And *eureka*, he woke to find her scrubbing the floors with a rag soaked in Clorox. Purging the mudroom of a thousand paper bags, so for the first time in forever the space didn't pass as a firetrap. Organizing her shoes and clothes with the precision of a poodle groomer. If that wasn't enough *hallelujah* for one lifetime, later that night while eating a proper meal together for the first time in weeks, Pierre let it out that he'd begun to remember. As proof, he recited what he'd done for the last two hours in minute detail, which took a good twenty minutes. Celine went completely apeshit. They group-hugged and this time meant it. And though Claude was glad to have his wife functioning again—sex twice in subsequent days—and Pierre back to his preadolescent, quirky self, he couldn't trust it. Something nagged at him. Something he didn't know about. Or had forgotten. He should have been happy, or at least relieved. But sitting on the john at the hospital, Claude couldn't locate those emotions.

He groaned. The piss he'd been holding back finally sputtered into the toilet. He heard the men wash their hands and leave. And not a moment too soon, because not only did his shit let loose but worse, Claude began to cry. Embarrassing, racking, heaving sobs. During which he remembered that on the drive to the hospital that morning Pierre had explained the big bang to him and predicted that in their lifetime this would be replaced by some new theory. And for all his caution and covering of tracks, Claude now worried that he too would be exposed as out-of-date, and replaced. He opened the stall door and saw his puffy face, his hair like a zombie, his eyes haunted. Claude barely recognized the creature in the mirror.

Celine and Pierre, Edna, and the Kimbrough duo would be waiting for him in the cafeteria. Claude had been the last to donate, and he was surprised to see that between the bloodletting and his bathroom break-down, over an hour had passed. After throwing water on his face, he hurried back down the corridor, passing the nurse who now ignored him. All at once a bunch of doctors clustered around him, blocking his path. One, whom he recognized as the head honcho of hematology, grabbed him by the arm and hustled him into a large office with a huge desk and tons of bookshelves and walls smattered with degrees and citations and probably even the bronze Medal of Freedom. The doctor impatiently gestured for Claude to sit in a too-small chair, then towered over him from behind his desk. The positioning made Claude feel puny and trapped. Guilty as charged.

"We've been looking for you," the doctor said, pushing his glasses up onto his bald head.

"Yeah?" Dear God, Claude thought. How could this doctor know?

"Mr. Roy, did you know you have AB negative blood?"

"Not really. Maybe . . . no," Claude stammered with confusion.

"It's the rarest type."

"So?"

"The reason I mention this is that Luc Sibley also has AB negative."

"*So?*"

"Does that mean anything to you?"

"Why would it?" Claude didn't like the tone from this know-it-all and sat back, crossing his arms.

"One of the reasons we're having trouble getting Luc matched is that we discovered he also has an atypical antigen in his blood. The people we've tested who have AB negative don't have that antigen and so aren't close enough matches. But you have both. Which makes you a very close match."

"Okay, okay," Claude said, annoyed. "I'll give more blood. That what you want?"

"Well yes, that would be expected, of course. But you should know that only a relative could match the way you have . . . with such specificity."

"Uh-uh, no," Claude said, shaking his head. "No. We're not related. No."

"What I'm trying to tell you, Mr. Roy, is that you *are* related."

"Not possible," Claude whispered to himself.

He jumped up out of his chair, causing it to slam into the bookcase. He backed against the closed door, trying to gain distance from the doctor and the entire subject.

"This is not possible," he repeated, this time louder than he meant.

"Science doesn't lie," the doctor responded quietly, now sitting at his desk with his hands folded.

Claude sat back down and wiped his nose on his sleeve. Blood. The doctor handed him a paper-towel square and Claude blew furiously, examined the mess, and balled it into his fist. He scanned the wall again and now saw that the awards were mostly for the guy's kid, his scholastic achievements, soccer-team wins, a spelling bee.

"Have you told anyone?" Claude asked, still staring at the wall.

"This is a privileged conversation."

"What do you want?"

"Give us more blood now. We'll make sure Luc can tolerate it as we suspect he will. Then we'll ask you to come in again. Could be as soon as tomorrow."

"Just get on with it," Claude said for the second time that morning.

The big shot drew the blood himself. A real pro, he didn't bother with flicking his fingers at Claude's elbow or the fist-squeezing routine. While the blood drained from Claude's vein, they passed the time talking about the doctor's kids. One had skipped a grade in junior high because he was superbright, but was having a hard time adjusting emotionally. The younger had recently been diagnosed with autism spectrum, and his wife had quit her job to care for him full time. Claude found himself warming to this man and was thinking about disclosing Pierre's memory loss and recent recovery, maybe buck the guy up a bit. But the conversation came to an abrupt halt because the bag was full. The doctor pressed a cotton ball onto the second puncture in Claude's arm, then handed him the roll of paper towels.

"Apply pressure to that," the doctor advised, pointing to Claude's nose, which had begun to drip again, then sprinted out of the room.

Claude found them all wedged into a corner of the cafeteria. Saint Sandra was just returning with drinks on a tray. Jim and Celine sat at opposite ends of the table, both reading different sections of the Oslo *Penny Saver*.

"That took a long time, Dad. What happened?" Pierre asked without looking up from his book.

"I got a bloody nose and couldn't get it to stop."

"That's weird," Pierre mused, and continued reading.

Claude sat next to Edna, who barely registered his arrival. She wore a dowdy housedress with a limp scarf around her shoulders. No lipstick. Her hands quivered as she continually wiped her eyes with a handkerchief.

"Why didn't I call the police that night?" Edna groaned, ignoring the cup of tea Sandra had placed in front of her.

"Nothing you could have done would have made a difference," Sandra said. "Not even calling the police. They'd never have found him. Just thank God that guy happened to wander out for a smoke when he did. Come on. The tea will feel good."

Sandra began to spoon sugar into Edna's cup, when the hematologist approached.

"Mrs. Sibley, we have good news."

"You *do*?"

"We found a very close match. Luc's receiving the blood now."

"Who is it?" Sandra asked.

"The donor wants to remain anonymous," the doctor responded quickly, avoiding Claude's stare. "But since Luc isn't in danger anymore, I suggest you go home and get some rest."

"But I want to *be* with him," Edna pleaded.

"There's nothing to be gained by staying. We'll call you immediately if there are any changes. But I'm fairly confident that Luc will regain consciousness before too long."

After much cajoling, Jim convinced Edna to go to lunch with him. Celine asked Sandra to come back to the house and help her sort through the kitchen pantry. That left Claude in the cafeteria with Pierre, who continued to read his book and sip a Coke with a cherry at the bottom of the glass.

"Don't eat that cherry, son," Claude advised.

Pierre looked up, suspicious. "Luc eats them."

"True. But I know for a fact that Mrs. Kimbrough says they stay in your stomach for an entire *year*."

"Actually, it's only a week. She warned me, too." Pierre heaved a great sigh, licked his finger, and turned a page.

"How's about you and me go back to the house and on the way, you can tell me all about this book you can't get your snout out of," Claude suggested.

Pierre looked at him as if he were an alien. "Really? You probably won't like it."

"I'll risk it."

While Claude drove, Pierre told him the story of a pathetic fisherman from Cuba who hadn't caught a fish in eighty-four days. He kept interrupting the plot with asides about what the fisherman wore and how he navigated the sea. Claude, of course, had no real interest in the unnecessary details or even the story. But he stayed quiet and feigned curiosity because he only wanted his son near him. Once Pierre finished with the recap, he began reading straight from the book. His voice, though still high, cracked now and then. This was something Claude hadn't noticed before. He looked over and saw small but undeniably dark and coarse hairs on the boy's calves. Innocence was almost over, and Claude pulled his son close. Pierre then began to yawn, and let the book drop from his hands. His head landed in Claude's lap, and Pierre was asleep in a few seconds.

They were almost home now. He'd just passed the Kimbrough house on the right and began down the slope to his own home. Midway, he stopped the car and idled. The camp he'd forbidden Pierre to attend sat empty. Claude had attended one summer when he was fifteen, intent on playing baseball as much as possible. He was a talented athlete, a better-than-decent hitter, and dominated the first-base defensive position with his quick reflexes. The Red Sox were a big topic all summer, and late into the night while lying in their bunks, the boys debated endlessly about the season in nearby Boston. And there were other obsessions. Masturbation of course, which then naturally led to the topic of sex. Pierre squirmed in his sleep. Claude placed his hand on the boy's forehead. It felt cool and dry. He looked at the open field on the opposite side of the road, with tall grasses and trees beyond. Not much had changed since that summer when a plan had been hatched. It seemed there was a girl, and she was willing.

On the last night of the camp session, in the middle of this very field, Claude drank until he could barely stand. He'd never swallowed even one drop of alcohol before. Nor had he held a girl's hand, much less kissed one on the cheek. But he went first. And with the blessing of his first alcohol blackout, Claude woke the next morning not remembering what had happened or who the girl was. Not even her first name. Claude was still an innocent, like his boy who now slept so deeply.

He shifted into drive and continued down the hill. Pierre woke up when they turned into the driveway and parked. Celine and the Saint walked out of the house carrying boxes of shoes worth too much money. They stacked them on the floor of the porch, preparing for donation the next day.

"Jim just called," Sandra announced. "Edna wants us all for dinner tonight."

"It's *Feud* night!" Pierre said, jumping up and down. "We can watch together. It'd be kind of cool. Luc would like that."

Pierre sat next to Claude on the steps to the front porch as Celine re-examined each pair of shoes, displaying the outlandish styles and gaudy colors, marveling at the heels. Then she put on a pair she felt a particular fondness for and pranced around the front lawn. Pierre giggled at the spectacle and Celine, for the first time in what felt like forever, seemed truly happy. The wind blew across Claude's face and he closed his eyes to its warmth. But really, he didn't want to see the joy his family had finally located. Because Luc Sibley was his son.

RACHEL

MOSTLY, THINGS WERE BACK TO NORMAL.
The house smelled both clean and delicious. Pierre's mom had been
cooking lots of meals—dinner *and* lunch. A good thing too, because
he was tired of tuna-fish sandwiches four days a week and bologna and
mustard the other three. And his parents seemed to like each other again.
At least they weren't arguing in his mom's bedroom and acting as if he
couldn't hear every other sentence. In fact, that room was now being used
for storage while his mom sorted out which fancy shoes and clothes (that
she'd never worn) would go to Goodwill. She said she wanted to pare
down her life—*clarify* things. Whatever that meant. But nothing at all,
in any way, was clear. Because Luc was sick, and Pierre wasn't sure with
what. All week long he'd asked for details, but the adults did what they
always do. Without explaining anything, they told him not to worry. That
wasn't fair, because Pierre liked Luc. He was funny on *Feud* night and
could remember a million details about lots of old TV shows. But while
Luc was in his coma no one was allowed to be funny, and it seemed like it
was wrong to laugh or even smile. Then yesterday, there was good news.

The morning had dragged on forever, what with his dad's donation taking extra long due to his bloody nose. Luckily, Pierre's book passed the time and was a good distraction from Edna crying on and off and Mrs. Kimbrough trying to *calm* her with about twenty cups of tea. Which Pierre didn't get, because wasn't tea full of caffeine? His mom spent the entire time consulting with Mr. Kimbrough about sales on gardening tools, which also made no sense because his mom didn't even like plants. But then they got the news about Luc's blood, so Pierre hoped things might *finally* go back to normal.

But there was always something. Very early this morning his dad woke him before it was light out to say they were going to get breakfast at the diner with Edna. Pierre couldn't see his dad's face very well, because he'd not turned on the light. But he did notice his dad wore sunglasses. Which was strange, because not only was the room pretty dark, but his dad always said that people who wore sunglasses were probably liars. He kept adjusting the frames up and down his nose with his thumb and had to clamp his hand shut to keep his fingers from shaking. That's when Pierre realized things might not be as normal as he'd wished.

After the sun came up, they stood by the door getting ready to leave, and his mom asked him for the millionth time if he'd be okay alone in the house while they went for breakfast with Edna. And Pierre answered for the billionth time, yes, he'd be fine. She'd never been concerned the other times he'd stayed home alone. Not like this, anyway. Pierre watched them walk to the car. His dad got in on the passenger side, his mom in the driver seat. His dad always, *always* drove. And for the first time ever, Pierre felt more worried for his dad than for his mom.

As his memory had continued to improve, everyone assured him this was positive. But Pierre didn't like that he couldn't control what memories popped up. Some were fine. Like the Ringleader's real name was Rachel, and she also studied violin with Mrs. Kimbrough. Others weren't so good. Like remembering that late last night when he'd peeked into the kitchen he saw his parents hovering over his mom's computer. His mom was saying, *it's okay, it's okay,* over and over. And then again at three a.m. His mom was sitting in his dad's lap with her arms around him. This time they didn't talk. And Pierre now understood the sunglasses because he also remembered that his dad was crying but trying to not make any sounds. His dad wasn't a liar—he'd just wanted to hide his puffy eyes.

Pierre had spent the morning lying on his bed thinking about all these things when the phone in the kitchen rang. He usually let it go, but he was worried it might be his mom calling to see if he was okay.

"Is Claude Roy at home?" a woman with a high voice asked.

"He's out."

"Can you give him a message?"

"Sure."

"I'm calling from Franklin County General, the hematology department. Dr. Litvak needs to schedule another blood donation from Mr. Roy. Please have him call as soon as he gets this message."

"Um, okay."

"You'll give him the message? It's important," the woman squeaked.

"He'll be home soon. I think."

Pierre hung up the phone. He pushed an ashtray overflowing with stubs to the side. That Litvak guy said the donor with the correct blood for Luc was *anonymous*. His dad wasn't anonymous. Pierre decided to check the exact meaning of that word. He opened his mom's laptop, still on the kitchen table from the night before, and googled.

A·non·y·mous—*A person not identified by name. As in an anonymous donor. Secret. Incognito.*

No. It couldn't be his dad. He wasn't a secret. His dad was practically famous in Oslo . . . but what was *incognito*?

In·cog·ni·to—*Having one's true identity concealed.*

If his dad's blood was good for Luc, why were they hiding it? Pierre sipped on a Coke, trying to make sense of the words and what they meant about his dad. Then his stomach growled from hunger and he realized he'd not eaten breakfast yet, so he grabbed two bananas from the fruit bowl and spent another minute munching and thinking. The computer screen saver suddenly appeared—an embarrassing picture of him as an infant. Pierre quickly rubbed the trackpad to get rid of it. Then on impulse, he hovered the arrow over the history tab. His finger froze. He'd never been snoopy like some of his friends, searching through closets and drawers and then discovering creepy things they'd rather not know about their parents. His mom inspected his laptop history all the time, but that's just what all the moms did. And anyway, Pierre's history only showed YouTube videos of the great violinists. Lots of book browsing. And wiki searches of people like Aristotle and Camus and Shostakovich and Hemingway and Neil deGrasse Tyson. Nothing bad. What he'd been careful to delete every single day were searches for boarding schools with good music departments, which Pierre was curious about but knew they could never afford. And summer music festivals that Mrs. Kimbrough said were actually possible the next year because he'd improved so quickly and could get a scholarship. Then, music conservatories for after high school, an idea he didn't dare share with anyone, not even Mrs. Kimbrough. If his mom knew he wanted to leave home, that would hurt her feelings and she might go all sloppy again.

Pierre clicked. The tab dropped down. As soon as the list appeared, he drew his hands back as if the keyboard had caught fire. Dozens and dozens of searches appeared from the night before on just two subjects. First, AB negative blood. They'd been talking about this all week long and Pierre understood it was rare, which was why Luc wasn't getting better. Second, *paternity*. Pierre didn't have to look that word up. He already knew the meaning because at the end of the school year his class had learned about family trees and tracing ancestry through DNA. Pierre slammed the computer shut, ran to his bedroom, and dove onto the bed.

Now. Now. Now. Now. Now. Repeating the word out loud didn't work. He pressed the heels of his palms against his eyes. *Don't cry.* He drew his knees to his chest and squeezed. *Don't remember.* He rocked back and forth. *Don't wish.* He clenched his fists and toes. *Don't even think.* About anything. His head began to pound and he felt slightly sick to his stomach. Pierre rolled to his side and landed with his nose about five inches from the scroll of his violin, the smell of the varnish woody and oily. He drew its human shape into the crook of his body. *Trust only this.*

Tires crunched over the gravel outside. Pierre ignored his physical discomfort and quickly grabbed his violin. He stood in the middle of the room and began to draw his bow across the strings. Back and forth, over and over. He tried to remember every single thing Mrs. Kimbrough had taught him, all at once. He concentrated on pitch and smoothness of sound and his bow arm. He thought of how a beautiful melody could stay in his head for days. Then he imagined the sound entering his body and hoped it would stay there forever. Just then, the door opened and they rustled into the room. He felt their bodies taking up space, their eyes on his back as they waited for him to turn around. But Pierre kept his eyes shut and played louder, forcing the bow hard onto the string. He even made an ugly sound Mrs. Kimbrough wouldn't like, but he didn't care. He would play and play and play for as long as it took. Because Pierre ached for the *now*.

Then, he sensed a set of hands on his shoulders, the touch light, like a bird. And somehow, he knew it was Edna. "Dear boy," she said, and kissed the back of his head. Those two words and the sound of her voice and the feeling of her lips brushing against his hair made Pierre shiver. It was a pleasurable spasm, so much so that he stopped playing his violin.

When he opened his eyes and turned around, he saw his dad kneeling on the floor by the door, his mom standing behind. Edna squeezed him tight, her arms now strong in a way that Pierre knew was safe. He closed his eyes again and breathed in her sweater, which smelled of roses. He saw pink and laughed. Then he tasted sweetness. Now, he could finally cry. Pierre rubbed his tears against Edna's chest, needing, needing, needing her smell. There they were. The roses.

Then, there it was.

The *now*.

EPILOGUE

EDNA SIBLEY DIES WITHIN THE YEAR. IT turns out she was, as everyone in Oslo suspected, filthy rich, and her will sustains her grandson comfortably. Luc quits his job at the March and continues to live in the house on the lake, though formal dining never graces the Sibley table again. He occupies his time on all the social-media platforms as a way to communicate in his odd manner. Eventually, he moves exclusively to Twitter with the handle @whatmygramsaid. Luc's daily tweets about what his gram said garner millions of likes and retweets. He, and Gram, trend regularly.

Jim quits the symphony and Sandra sells his cello to pay off all their debts. Now without an instrument, Jim devotes himself to his real passion in life: solar panels. Within a year, he develops a system that revolutionizes the solar-panel industry. He sells the invention to a startup, netting a hefty sum. As Jim settles in as full-time househusband and fixer-upper, Sandra uses some of the solar money to buy the land across from their house, where the campground once stood. She starts a music camp for underprivileged children in Maine. And though she and Jim are now fairly well-off, Sandra continues teaching violin to the kids of Oslo. Her students, year after year, attend conservatories throughout the country and populate orchestras around the world.

Claude never publicly acknowledges Luc as his son, something that Celine, Sandra, and Jim respect and accommodate. A codicil attached to Edna's will, written a week before she dies, provides a modest income for Claude and Celine if and when the March goes belly up, which it does within a few years. Claude continues to add to the footprint of his house, with challenging logic. Celine stays off the pills for the most part, slipping only twice. She passes away in her sleep at the age of fifty-one, of heart disease. Sandra remains her best friend till the end. Claude, bereft, never remarries.

Of course, Pierre marries Rachel the Ringleader, who was Sandra's other prize student. They attend conservatory together, thanks to financial help from Edna's will, and then move to Boston to begin their performing careers. Pierre soon abandons the ambition because tremors induced by the kick from the moose continue to plague him and ultimately interfere with his ability to perform consistently. Instead, Pierre builds a teaching studio in Boston and becomes one of the most important pedagogues in the country. He's known as "the bow-arm fixer." Professional violinists from around the world run to Pierre when their bow arms are in trouble, all thanks to the fundamentals Sandra developed in him when he was young. Rachel tours as first violinist with a well-established and successful string quartet. Sandra is named godmother to their two children, Luc and Edie. When Pierre and Rachel are able to purchase a two-family brownstone in Back Bay, Boston, they move Claude into the bottom residence. He co-parents the kids with Pierre while Rachel is away on tour and manages to tolerate the Saint when she visits, which is, to his mind, too often.

When his children are still small, Pierre tells them fantastical stories about the people who live in a Maine town called Oslo. He tells them their Uncle Luc is brilliant and can recite verbatim all 198 episodes of *Family Feud*, the Richard Dawson years. He tells them their Grandma Celine was a quiet and kind beauty, who all her life bought and donated shoes to the poorest of Oslo. He tells them they must listen to their Grandpa Claude, but not too much. He tells them their Auntie Sandra taught him and Mommy how to play the violin and that she actually *is* a saint, just as Grandpa Claude calls her. And, he tells them about an old lady named Edna who smelled like a pink rose and is the reason they always use cloth napkins at the dinner table. Pierre promises that one day in the future, he'll tell them all about a moose and how she brought him to understand the beauty of *now*. But when they say, "Daddy, tell us about the moose. Tell us now about the *now*," Pierre cannot, for the life of him, find the words.

END

ACKNOWLEDGEMENTS

I am honored to be published, once again, by Michelle Halket. Her continued belief in my work is a writer's dream. I'm grateful for her confidence and strategic thinking, particularly in very trying times. Many thanks to the sales team at IPG who distributed my novel with imagination and enthusiasm. My exceptional publicist, Sheryl Johnston, guided me with sensitivity throughout.

The Virginia Center for the Creative Arts generously provided two residencies in one calendar year where I was able to complete a first draft. Céleste-Marie Roy lent me her studio in Switzerland for the better part of a summer. What a joy to write in seclusion with Lake Geneva just down the block.

Early chapters of *Oslo, Maine* were workshopped with Zeeva Bukai, Julia Hirsch and Rosanne Limoncelli. Ralph Olsen, my forever go-to, read multiple versions throughout. Beta readers Patty Dann, Amy Kathleen Ryan and Don Shaw reviewed a later draft. I am indebted to all these wonderful friends and writers who took time and trouble to read my words and give invaluable feedback and encouragement. A writer can't do it alone. I am very lucky.

Photo: Matt Dine

Marcia Butler, a former professional oboist and interior designer, is the author of the memoir, *The Skin Above My Knee*, and debut novel, *Pickle's Progress*. With her second novel, *Oslo, Maine*, Marcia draws on indelible memories of performing for fifteen years at a chamber music festival in central Maine. While there, she came to love the people, the diverse topography, and especially the majestic and endlessly fascinating moose who roam, at their perpetual peril, among the humans. After many decades in New York City, Marcia now makes her home in Santa Fe, New Mexico.